BUXTON SPICE

Oonya Kempadoo

BUXTON SPICE

PHOENIX HOUSE
London

First published in Great Britain
in 1998 by Phoenix House

Typeset at The Spartan Press Ltd,
Lymington, Hants
Printed by Butler & Tanner Ltd,
Frome and London.

Phoenix House
Weidenfeld & Nicolson
The Orion Publishing Group Ltd
Orion House, 5 Upper Saint Martin's Lane
London, WC2H 9EA

To Roger and Sonan

ONE

I got to know all the secrets of the house – like I knew all the trees in the yard. Flipped over the back of the Morris chair, my head sunk into the seat, I spent a long time walking on the smooth ceiling, stepping over the little partitions in the upside-down doorways and sitting on the fretwork. No furniture cluttered those rooms. No dust. And if I wanted, I could even fill up a room with water to make it a pool.

The white paint that flaked off the windowsills would stick to my chin and the undersides of my arms. And the bare grey wood smelt sweet like skin, not mouldy like the black skirting board by the bathroom that was always damp and eaten away at the bottom. Morning sun made long dazzling doorways on the polished living-room floor that shrank slowly until only the dwarfs could pass through them. As I swept the floor in the morning light, the dust would just rise up and float twinkling out the windows. The broom stroked every plank, some of them slightly rounded, some dark; some had a hole in them, perfectly round to peep through. All smooth. So smooth my sister could pull my feet and I'd slide fast till my bum got hot or my skirt slipped up and I stopped with a squeaky bump. But other parts of the floor – where the putty had come out – you couldn't even play jacks on and my broom could never get the dust out of those cracks.

Start by the screen door to the kitchen, sweeping across the planks not along them, rippling past the big bookshelf – sweep, sweep, sweep, stamp the broom. Sweep, sweep, sweep, stamp, stamp. Then into my mother's room – bed always made up with the blue knitted spread with little bumps that you could sit and pick off if you had something serious to discuss. Sweep, sweep, sweep, stamp. Join up with the rest of the dust by the armchair. Sweep, sweep, sweep, stamp, stamp. Stop by the hanging womb-chair. Middle bedroom had a bunk bed and some tentesse shelves, packed with my brother's things – wires, pieces of radio. Smelt of chemicals, salts and burnt copper. Sweep, sweep, sweep, stamp. Past the built-in shelves and the rows of paperbacks, most of them poetry, orange-cover Penguin classics, books about Buddhism and Zen. The small front room belonged to our househelp Miss Mary. Didn't have to stroke the floor in there. She didn't like no one going in. Always burning candles, wailing and praying.

Now *along* the floorboards. Through all the dazzling doorways by the windows. The sssweep of the broom going slow, flicking at the end, before the stamp. Now the dust floated differently. You could see it touching the glistening arms of the chairs and the edge of the low polished table – just touching gently before drifting away. Push into the corner of the living room, by the stairbox, where more

4

bookshelves sagged with encyclopedias and an aquarium. Magazines and old newspapers from Cuba piled up to the windowsills. Light coming through the frosted panes made the whole corner bright. Sweep, sweep, sweep, stamp, stamp – between the iron legs of the sewing machine and around the corner to the big empty centre of the room where the dust trap lay. Fold back the Tibisiri straw mat and the gleam of the floor disappeared. A steady sweep, stamp, sweep, stamp, now, to shift the lazy dust. Made it satisfying, though, replaced the happy flecks that had floated up and out. Sweep, stamp, sweep, stamp, the other half. Now all the dusty creeks joining the main river to flow past the settee and down the steps into the dark depths at the bottom of the front door.

The river runs easy – me standing with my feet in it, sliding it along every step and on to the one below. At the bottom, stamp and climb out of it. Now standing above it, hitting the door with the broomhead, frothing up the river on the last darkest step. And now fling open the door – saving everyone from the flood. See how much dust flying. Everything just disappearing in the hot bright light. The dust that can't fly, melting into the bare concrete steps, some slipping off the edge. Even my skin, damp with sweat, disappeared that dust. And the rest settled in the crevices of my big toes between dull nail and skin.

Tamarind Grove had four mad people. Uncle Joe was the safe one, the soft madman. He could help you with any homework, sums or spelling. When school over, children in blue uniforms would clump up around him by the roadside. Soon as they read out the sum, he'd be whispering the answers. Grubby little hands, gripping stubs of lead pencils flying over the exercise page, would fill in the numbers. And spelling. Any word you call he could spell. Some children'd be poking him, prodding him, pulling his shirt, calling out words while others tried more sums.

Big people called out even bigger words – trying to find him wrong. Uncle Joe was never wrong. Bright. Genius we'd say. Years ago he'd been postmaster, studied so hard he went off. You could see the signs of studying too. His left wrist had a big lump – big as a ping-pong ball – where he used to brace his head on it. And his right hand, the pen-gripping fingers, had plenty corns. Thick and hard. Grown there from writing too much. Too many hours gripping that pen tight must send a man off. And for some reason, Uncle Joe couldn't talk loud or even normal any more, only whisper. Must be the self-same reason made him smile all the time and shake his head to the side. Always trying to be nice. If your basket too heavy coming home from market – he'd take it gently out'a you hand and carry it. If you step out'a taxi on Mainroad in blazing sun, loaded down with bags and a sleeping child, he'd carry the bags all the way home and never ask for money. You dropped a dollar and didn't know it – he'd scramble up from the dust some-where, and chase you down to give it back, bowing and scraping all the time. People gave him food, cigarettes, money. He'd never take rum. Sometimes he'd come in the yard and sweep the whole bottom-house, wash down the open drains and, if nobody was around, he'd eat the rice left over in the dog's bowl. Made you shamed when he did that though, wished you was around to give him a sandwich or some sugar water.

Today he eat and done already. When we came down from lunch, the four a'we girls, he was sprawled-off under the house, snoring on the in-breath, he two knees crooked and flapped open, his stain-up khaki pants taut between them. In the middle of his crotch, where the stitching had bust, was a lovely big hole, just skinning up at us. Straight there we headed, pushing and jostling, gulping down our squeals and squeaks to get a better look, peeping down that hole into the darkness of his pants. Inside, the curve barely visible, was a wrinkled, wrinkled, thick dull brown almost black skin. A few glints showed was hair there too. Plenty behind the curve and some curling out of the balls. Wasn't like no skin I'd ever seen. Too thick and wrinkly, not smooth and shining like my brother's young balls. To see them good, you had to lean right down and hold your breath. One thing Uncle Joe didn't like doing was bathing. And from that hole, Uncle Joe's pure smell came straight at you. That real vagrant smell – sweat, pee, stale cigarettes and crotch smell. Was that made you know he was mad too. Gasping for breath and pushing to take turns, we skinned-teeth like fools, blubbering around on the ground. My hand clamped over Rachel's mouth, my sleeve wet from corking my own bawling. Judy collapsed, she couldn't take it no more. Stupidy grinning face, red and shaking, she jammed Uncle Joe's foot. His legs clapped shut so fast. One hand fly down to his crotch and he sitting up straight now, rubbing his boo-boo eyes with the other hand. We was just rolling. Stamping and slapping the ground. Running up and down in front of him. Holding on to each other and folding up laughing like we had hinges everywhere. When his red eyes could see, he started laughing too, legs straight out in front of him clamped tight. His sideways, shake-head laugh. Making five of us in the foolishness under the bottom-house.

*

7

The front room downstairs had a stale piano, a baby grand – the third leg a packing chest and the cover cracked. In this yellow room, even on the hottest, driest day the pungent smell of damp newsprint, books and mouse-eaten felt lay like a blanket floating at the height of the windowsills – sliding out when you opened the front doors. Piles of music books, cardboard boxes, wooden chests and crates were the piano's only audience. All underneath the piano was packed with audience. The only empty space left in the room was an L-shaped piece of pocky concrete floor.

'Ann, Uncle Joe. Ann. Remember she?'

'She coming back from Suriname just now you know.'

'You like she nuh, you wicked t'ing you.'

'Ow, Uncle Joe – how you could like a big-shot girl like dat?'

Uncle Joe's aroma wafted around the piano room, mixing with the book and mouse-eaten felt smell. Sammy stood gripping the lock of the front door, eye open big – supposed to be locking him in with us and everybody else out but looked like she was going to run away any minute. I guarded the other door that led to the middle room. We had him cornered in the far end of the L space, against the piano. We was the ones frightened though, while he was gently dreaming of Ann, shifting slowly from foot to foot, still holding his embarrassed crotch.

'Yes, Uncle Joe. You like she. Ah know you like she. Oh me gawd, what you would do wid a nice girl like dat?'

That tickled him by one of his kidneys. He ginched and giggled jerkily.

'Youall mustn't be talking bout Miss Ann like dat,' he squeaked. 'Miss Ann is a decent lady. I like Miss Ann too bad.'

'Well what you would do bout it, if she liked you too?'

He jumped again, smiling wider. 'Liked me? If she liked me?'

'Yes, Uncle Joe, she like you. I hear she say so already!'

'Marry she. She is a decent lady. I would marry she.'

He whispered it over and over softly, rocking himself.

'But Uncle Joe, what you would do *after* you marry she? What you would do, eh?'

His head snapped up and his eyes scanned our faces. The worried flash faded from his face and he grinned at us.

'Youall are very wicked. Wicked chi'ren. Not nice.' Wincing it out but smiling his shake-head smile all the time.

'We not asking you to do no wickedness, Uncle Joe. Just show we what you would do to Ann after you marry she. Just show we, dat's all.'

'You want to see what I would do to Miss Ann?'

'Yes. Yes . . . the piano is Miss Ann.'

He turned round to the piano, leaning his waist against it, stroking the curve of its belly, muttering 'Miss Ann? Miss Ann?'

We touching the piano now too, crowded up by the keyboard end.

'Miss Ann?' He bent down slowly, rested his dry lips on the wood, rubbed them in an arc on her chest, stroking her side with his hand.

'Ow Miss Ann,' his voice trembling.

'What he doing?'

'Sssh! You can't see is kiss he kissing she?'

'Ow Miss Ann. Miss Ann sweet, eh?'

'You lolo, Uncle Joe. What you would do wid your *lolo*?'

'Un humh? Miss Ann is a nice lady, eh?' His head hung right down on his chest while he caressed that piano cover.

9

We could see the bulge of his khaki lolo growing between him and the smooth wood – just kept pushing up till it was straining at the string tied round his waist. He kept polishing.

'Uncle Joe, what's dat? All dat's lolo? Miss Ann would like dat!'

'Ow Miss Ann. Miss Ann nice, eh?'

'Take it out, Uncle Joe, take it out!'

'Uh huh. Nice Miss Ann.' He was still stroking her and now himself too. Scrubbing down his pants from the top of his lolo, with the heel of his palm. The zip had long gone and the front only lapped over, held down by the string. He reached in and brought his hand back out holding one huge thing.

'Waagh! Donkey lolo!' Never seen a big man's lolo, much less one this huge, much less one this black, much less this close. Just kept looking. He held it like it didn't belong to him.

'Donkey lolo! Donkey lolo!' Wasn't far from donkey lolo, stretched skin, with a dark sheen, pulled back behind the head the same way. Nodding the same way too, but hanging up instead of hanging down. Looked like it was moving by itself. Uncle Joe didn't even know what to do with it, with his embarrassed self. He watched it like us. As we all stared, it went down slowly. Right there in his hand, it shrivelled and got more black, till he was weighing it, bouncing it with a smacking sound in his palm and smiling his shake-head smile.

'This is what Miss Ann would like? Nice Miss Ann?' Pinching in his bumsey, he pressed the end of his soft lolo against her, pushing the loose skin up with his fingers. We scrambled round the side to see the smudge it left on the

10

wood. A new scent blended with that acid afternoon air. His dry hand rasping on mahogany was the only sound in the room now.

'Youall play the piano nuh? Come nuh, play. Make Miss Ann sing for me. Nice Miss Ann.'

We just had to. Made Miss Ann sing for one whole hour.

Up in the dungs tree, the one in the corner of the yard, was the conference room. The white undersides of the roundish leaves made rippling lace curtains that hid us just enough. The seating area was where the branches had no prickles but if you got up too quick prickles on the branch above juked you in you scalp. Was the Sweet Dungs Tree. The one to eat till you frothy inside. From here, me and my sister Sammy and Judy and Rachel DeAbro, we kept an eye on the DeAbros' verandah across the side street and on the Bakers' empty front steps. Watched and waited for Mikey, Neighbour Mildred's son, to pass. Between conferences and watch duties, we'd see whose pee could dig the deepest hole in the dirt below. Squatting and hanging on, strung along one branch, we'd try to start peeing at the same time. Judy's spurt always shot out the furthest until our drilling, puddling sounds trailed off. When it had just rained, little puffs of steam drifted away from the warm pee holes, gone by the time we scrambled down to inspect them.

Run like rats from one tree to the next. Race down the Sweet Dungs trunk and up the Male Genip Tree. It couldn't bear nothing but it played with us – bending down its branches to reach the ground. Sliding you right down on your belly, smooth green bark on your thighs. But the Sweet Dungs Tree wouldn't budge. Not even move a prickle out of your way.

Over to the Bitter Dungs Tree. Underneath was smooth bare dirt and shade. Bumps on the big trunk, where its arms were trying to come out, was the only way up on to the main branch that spread level, high up above the dirt. All your jittering blood had to cool down now to reach up this one. Levering up, balancing with the smaller sister branch, made you feel warm, real proud to be there. The jittering slowly leaking out through your gripping fingertips into the branch. And the rough bark, pressing on your chestbone talking slow-down talk to your heart. The dirt looked far but not so far. If the tree talked to you long enough, you could jump right down. Just jump from squatting on that fat branch. Landing – knees snapping, palms slapping the ground. Stung you seconds after, from your soles slowly up to your head till you realized you did it.

Liming by the chicken coop under the starapple tree. Idling where you couldn't be seen from the kitchen window. That cool starapple tree in the middle of the yard. Tall so, taller than the kitchen. Leaves so pretty, like the leaves of October in the Canada almanac. Gold, orange, purple, green. This is Dreamers Tree. Lying on the warm chicken coop galvanize, I would fly up through those stiff, dry leaves, brushing off gold dust. Sit down on a twiggy branch next to a big Kisskadee bird cleaning starapple stain off its beak. Rub up on a smooth green-skin fruit. Butt the shiny purple ones till they fall. The dry snap of a twig was the sound of magic crackling and glittering all around me. When I wasn't flying around in the tree and was human size again, I'd tap my little finger on them special bumpy knobs, the ones with a little hole in the centre. Waiting to see the magic come walking out.

'Get a hooker-stick.'

'No, the rake.' If you pelt them down with stones Dads sure to come out and holler on you.

Every year, the Small Mango Tree close to the kitchen drain fed us green mangoes without complaint till it was stripped. Not a blossom, not even a force-ripe mango was left. Wasn't a tree for liming or climbing, just one to pick from. Wasn't no fancy tree or a difficult tree but a bearing one. Hundreds of small green mangoes every season, plenty of them not getting a chance to ripen cause it was always one of the first trees in the village to bear. Everybody coming for 'two green mango' to make curry, or a dozen to make chow. We'd eat chow till we couldn't eat dinner – tongues hanging out and noses running from blazing pepper, lips purple with vinegar. The juice at the bottom of the bowl was the bestest part – dipping the mango seeds in and scraping till your teeth edged. Swigging it in turns, pushing your whole face in the plastic bowl, eyes smarting, stomach cramping. One day Sammy and Rachel decide they didn't get enough juice. They head off to the tofu store room and pull out the acetic acid. Didn't dilute it, figuring it would taste even better stronger. Mixed it with a little salt and pepper and downed bout half a cup each. If you hear bawl! Jumping up and down, stamping and holding they belly. We rush them upstairs and Mums start pouring water down their throats, shouting at them, they bawling and gurgling. More water. Big dipper-cupfuls, then milk and more milk. Their eyes streaming.

14

Sitting on the broad banister at the top of the steps in the kitchen, waiting for my sister's fudge to finish, I could feel the vibrating of the hand mill clamped on to the step in the room below.

'I coming back for some just now,' I told my sister.

Peeled my skin off the banister and crept down the steps. Idleness and wickedness made me hold my breath till I reached down to the door with the big bolt and nailed-on straps. I know Ramesh is on the other side, flop-hat pulled low, beginning to grind today's batch of soya beans. Pushing open the door enough to get my head through, I spot the top of his grey crimpline hat – his head stuck under the banister, right over the mill. He barely glanced at my foot – not surprised.

'Lu . . . la.' Going up at the end like my name was Indian.

I didn't answer, stopped the creeping and thumped down the rest of the steps. I lean-up on the cool pale green concrete wall, rocking myself so my whole back could touch it. Felt good on my bare shoulderblades and the backs of my arms. The fraying piece of jute sack I stood on started slipping slowly away from the wall. I didn't have to say nuthing – the mill talking now, loud and noisy. A big man eating and belching, chewing and talking at the same time. Soya paste came curling out from between the two grinding plates at the front of the mill, making a slimy, sticky, smacking-lips sound. The heavy rush of the mill handle – a rumbling, stomach-churning, teeth-gnashing sound. Chubby little beans tumbling into the gaping silver mouth of the cast-iron mill, rolled all around before being swallowed. I rocked slowly, watching Ramesh churning up these sounds and movements into a rhythm. Bringing cupful after cupful, pouring them slowly, never letting the mouth get empty. Them beans was hypnotizing in that mouth. Sucked down and then bumped back up. Glistening, cream-coloured fat beans with black belly-buttons. And a few that had bust out'a they skin and split themselves apart disappearing down the throat. The goo piled up in the plastic container tucked under the lips of the grinding plates. Piling and smacking, curling up until a lump tumbled down. Ramesh stopped to scrape the plates with a knife and level the pile.

'Mala making fudge,' I said, shifting to the windowsill close by.

'Uh huh.' Up at the end again, like it was interesting news but nothing to do with him. Like I just saying some stupidness again.

I sat myself on the windowsill, knees apart, wide enough to lift the hem of my skirt a little. He never looked directly at me when I talking to him. Always busying himself, finding something to do or something else to gaze at. I kept looking

16

at him. The top of his hat poked right under the banister. Couldn't see his eyes, only his long nose, the fuzz under it and his lips turned up a little in a half-smile. I smiled too. The two o'clock air thick with the milky, nutty smell of crushed beans and the room around us half dark. Shadows of sacks, baskets and buckets hunched against the wall behind him.

Ramesh worked around the yard – gardening, sweeping and making the tofu. I always watched his huge feet while he boiled the soya milk. Knew all their contours. Only his big toe touched the ground while he stood, and all his toes pointed in different directions, kept off the ground by well-padded soles with magnificent heels ending them off. Dads told me once that rice workers and people who does mind cows have duck-foot from walking in so much mud – spreads the toes apart and they stay so. Ramesh's toenails were square and outlined with dark mud. I knew how his feet sounded when they hit the concrete. When he ran he was a rooster – thudding past with arms crooked, wings slightly raised, chest puffed up and great heels spurring up behind.

But what I looking for now is new signs. Searching for signs on his chest, down to where his shirt was buttoned. And on his chin. Fine beads of sweat trembled in the fuzz above his lip and on his chest. I keep on staring. Among the baby hair holding the droplets to his skin was a few coarse black strands. And, on his chin – two! Just sprigging out. Bout half an inch long. Ridiculous things.

'Eh, eh boy! You ketch!' I screeched, jumping off the sill and pushing my face in front of the belching mill so I could see his eyes.

He brushed his chin with his shoulder, trying to hide his spreading smile.

17

'You get two hairs on yuh face!' I shouted over the noise, laughing like stupid. Pulled his hat right off. He stopped grinding and grabbed it back from me. Slapped my foot with it as I scuttled upstairs. The fudge cooling in the empty kitchen.

House quiet. Even the yard quiet. The heat of the day cooling to four o'clock feeling. Mums and Dads still resting. My sister Sammy helping Judy and Rachel DeAbro bag off sugar in their father's shop. Not me this afternoon. I slipped out the small front gate, four o'clock feeling inside me. Sun still too hot to move fast. Burnt my neck-back as I checked the cock-a-dung-guts fish in the open drain along our fence. Them little hungry things always looking for food, darting around, silver heads and see-through flashes against the smooth green silt. A pregnant one cruised past and I craned to see her eggs through her see-through sides. She didn't have no room for carrying around dung in her gut. Three stupid mosquito worms jiggled, giving themselves away. I straightened up. Looked around with my four o'clock feeling. Nobody on the street. Not a dog or fowlcock.

Slowly, I followed the drain along our greenheart paling. Grass springy and thick by the edge. Cannonball lilies always flowering, standing with their feet in the drain. Their blinding red heads the same height as the silver-grey paling points. Round the corner in the DeAbros' street, the drain rippled red with ringworm. On a hot afternoon like this, they'd just be swaying gently in the shallow water. The road was mostly smooth dirt, but a grassy patch gleamed grey with fresh wet mud where one of the pigs had been. I could see its head snouting in the drain further down by DeAbros' house. I skirted the pig mud carefully. Mums had tell me not to walk barefoot in mud like that cause of the hookworms. Sometimes you could see them if you spread pig mud on the street, fat white sausages with wiggling tails. I couldn't see how one a'them fat things could go through the skin on my foot-bottom without me feeling it. Made my feet itchy thinking bout it. Wasn't much sense in digging-up for them now, all by myself. Stretched to reach a branch that touched the water, shook it just a little bit. The ringworms wriggled away and quietly settled round a piece of moss.

I jumped over the drain and passed through the hole in the fence into the empty lot. Inside was only bush and two trees – a big genip tree in the middle and a cherry tree brace-up against the fence. I make for the cherry tree. The dry scratchy branches of blacksage bush scraped white lines on my shins. Made the afternoon feel hotter. Blacksage leaves crushed under my feet smelt like sweet wood. Poor man's toothbrush – if you broke off a stick and chewed the end. Strong, good for your gums. We tried it sometimes when we couldn't find fruits. This cherry tree was sometim-ish. This time, it hardly had much – just a few green ones. At least it had shade. Twiggy, dead-leaf-covered ground shade. But you still had to look out for broken bottles. People always pelted them into the lot to spite the owners who wasn't from Tamarind Grove. I looked closer at the shady ground to see if I could find any 'telling signs' – any of the DeAbros' old toothbrushes, bits of comb, a piece of hairbrush. I only found a dolly eye and some old blue plastic rosary beads. The green cherries bobbed on the tree, too high up for me to reach even with a stick. Went back through the scratchy blacksage and this time spotted some of the small red berries on the tip of one of the bushes. They just made a small taste in my mouth – wasn't as strong as the wood taste, mostly seed. I headed back to the big street. Four o'clock feeling fading. I left it right there by the top of DeAbros' street and went on up towards Scheme.

Some people was moving around now. Coming out of their streets. Boila wife came out their rumshop gate – going to DeAbro's shop with her oil bottle. The rumshop looked ridiculous in the day – bright turquoise with big black, yellow and red spots painted on the concrete front. Was always night inside there, painted black with pictures of girls on the walls but you could hardly see them. Boila rumshop was the only concrete building from Mainroad till Scheme. Mrs Boila was proud of that. When she quarrelled, she always ended up cussing people bout they ramshackle wooden houses.

Past the Harpers' house set back from the road and peeping out from behind a breadfruit tree. Wild dasheen leaves sprung out of the drain here, big and heart-shaped. Edges of the leaves rolled up and flashed their powdery white underneaths at me as I passed, bending and dancing on pale green stems as a slight wind picked up. Walking faster now. I moved on past Miss Isaac's house – so new the wood wasn't silver yet, still dark brown. She didn't have no empty bottom-house like most people. It was half enclosed and she kept her best cows in there. The damp wood soaked up the cow-dung smell so much, she'd never be able to get it out. The other cows slept outside in bruck-down pens. The whole of her muddy frontyard was cow-hoof holes. Deep ones. She laid planks so she could reach her bridge from her front step but the hooves trampled on them too, making them tip and twist, covering them in mud. Hoof holes fanned out from the bridge to the road edge. Sometimes them cows didn't bother with the bridge, just stamped through the drain while she tramped over the bridge, always hustling behind in her son's rubber boots.

Opposite her yard was the house with the longest front yard. Was where we went to buy fruitie ice blocks. Through the neat gate, along the two concrete strips set car-wheel width apart. Only two coconut trees rose out of that front yard – stretching higher than the house. Rich-looking grass carpet rolled out from the house with the car underneath, to the wire fence. Even between the concrete strips. Was what people called Lawngrass. The man had to have a Lawn-mower because of that grass and he showed it off every two weeks. I never could understand, though, why people rich so – with car and Lawngrass – had to sell ice blocks. Collecting our sweaty cents, filling up a glass bottle on top their fridge. Every time we climbed them steps up to the open half-door and stood and waited in the hot sun, I watched that bottle. What they needed them cents for? Peeping into the cool kitchen, listening for the girl to come, hearing her feet sticking on the clean lino floor, watching her clean hands taking out the ice blocks with a tongs and putting two into my palm, taking my six cents, dropping another block in my other palm – I knew they didn't really need them cents. Knew from the way she dropped them into the jar when we hustled away licking our dripping fists so it wouldn't sticky-up their spotless steps. That same girl scraped them steps every Saturday. Left them silky smooth and silver in the sun.

Past Look-Back's street now, to the skeleton of the sandbox tree at the end of the asphalt road. There, the drain turned its last corner into the last side street before the roughness and openness started under your feet and in the air. Breeze got stronger out here. I walked quicker. Half hobbling over the gravelly grass edge of the wide track. Lungs filled up with more space. Flat long-grass empty land. No more big trees now. The seawall in the distance was only a ribbon of grey. I knew where I was going now. To lie down on the one-plank bridge over Forty Canal and watch the Hassar catfish.

I laid myself right down along the plank. Shifted my shirt up so my belly could rest on the warm wood. Dangled my two plaits and long arms down, cheek warming too, searching the shallow edge of the canal for movement. Just below the surface, in the deep water centre, I saw them. Swimming like they had all the time in the world. Not cool, not hot. Just lukewarm like the water. Brown and milky like the water. Flexing their thick bodies, side to side, following their wide flat mouths. Long whiskers finning, smelling out things I couldn't see. The Smoking Hassar was darker, swimming deeper, almost a shadow.

Huge clouds swept over my back and rolled in towards home. The backs of my legs cooled. I swung my arms gently to see if the movement shooed the fish. They didn't take me on. Neither me nor the sudden wind that rippled the surface, making the water lick little kissing sounds in the corners by the reeds. They didn't bother if it was getting late or if it would rain tonight. They just didn't care.

That evening was rice and stew for dinner. Tofu and black-eye peas stew, pumpkin and bhagee.

'Pass the greens, Lula.'

I passed the bhagee. That's what Dads said this type of greens is called all over Guyana. I passed it along to Mala and she stretched over and passed it to Emanja who sat opposite her. Mums was at her end of the two tables put together and Dads at his end by the windows. This table used to hold more of us but the two eldest girls had long left home – gone back to England. My youngest sister Saskia sat squashed into her old high-chair next to Dads. On the other side of him my brother slouched on the built-in box of the kitchen staircase. He wouldn't let nobody else sit there cause the big biscuit tins were lined up just behind him. Biscuit King. Always trying to control the tins, rationing biscuits as if we had to beg him. And when he finished eating and said 'Excuse me from the table please' he'd bang the tins loud as he ran off. But only if Dads wasn't there.

Sammy and me looked at each other over the edges of our plates, measuring the lumps of bhagee on them by staring into each other's eyes. Sammy always gave trouble to eat. She'd pick at everything and then say how she was given more than me and she's smaller than me so how come she has to eat all. Dads was too far, way down the other end of the table, to know if was true. Mums just didn't take her on most times. Dads scooped the last of the pumpkin on to Saskia's and his plates.

'Waste not want not!'

He scraped it again even though it was empty. We were all looking at him, knives and forks ready. Waiting for him to put down the dish.

'This really looks good, Mums!'

We began eating.

'Look at all these colours on the plate. Look at this orange and green together.'

Saskia was busy tucking into the orange and the green, looking at him with a mouth full of agreement.

'You know, that's half the art of cooking, putting a lovely combination of colours together.'

In the pause everyone was chewing, sipping, gathering another forkful. A strong breeze sucked the air through the kitchen and made the fly screens stick on to the window-frames. Wisps of hair escaped from Dads's ponytail, lifted up and out. He stroked his long pointed beard and grinned at Mums.

'I think we'll have some rain tonight.'

From where I sat next to Mums, he looked so far away. Dark cool Madrasi, with his wisps flying around and white teeth and beard flashing at us. The V-neck of his cream shirt made his beard point down even more and his shoulders disappear against the cream wall. The lights were already on. Mums still looked rosy and warm from cooking. She smiled to herself at Dads's enthusiasm for the food and the weather. Freckles spotted her face and neck. Her bare orangey shoulders and arms were soft and round. That strong European nose, flat forehead, and the curve of her creole lips, held something from a gentle past. 'Bourgeois', Dads called her. She a convent schoolgirl when they met in Georgetown, he a young reporter. They got married long ago in New Amsterdam. Under her skin I could see the old-time features from the black and white wedding album pictures. Under Dads's skin too. And even though his hair was long now, beard turning grey, sometimes I saw the same smile pop out when he was teasing Mums, seeing how far he could go before she told him to stop talking foolishness.

Them old photos with misty soft faces and perfect skin. Mulatto women with smooth brows, full lips and wistful smiles, fine waists and small hands. Men posing wearing

24

baggy linen trousers, cricket clothes and oiled wavy hair. Square swimsuits worn with bumpy rubber swimcaps. Big rounded cars on English streets. Full skirts and bicycles in fields. Prams and babies with bonnets. Young Dads, hair crewcut, with white people and a big old BBC recording microphone, smiling. Mums answered the questions: who is who, what Dads was doing, what he did next, where the family went. But now, Dads's days was Uniting Nations. Found plenty to do after he read all them books in the house. Never had enough time in the day to make new projects so he was up at night too – pacing from the kitchen table to the front windows in his flip-flaps. Flip-flap. Flip-flap. Up and down. Then bang, bang, bang on his old Remington typewriter. I knew it was a Remington, the word was raised out of the bulbous metal front. Sometimes it sat there on the kitchen table, the base part of its box lined with bright green felt. Nobody was allowed to touch it. Dads was proud of it cause it was so old and still worked fine and because a lot of great writers had used Remington typewriters. I never knew what he typing so loud at nights. Work, Mums said. And it was his adrenalin glands working overtime that prevented him from sleeping. Sometimes she'd read his 'proposals' in the day while he paced and stroked his beard in front of her.

'What you going call this one?' Mums asked him now.

'Oh, I have a name already – "The Bantu Society".'

'What?'

'Oh yes! I've thought this through.'

'But that's African, Dads,' Mala objected. 'What does Africa have to do with Tamarind Grove?'

'The Bantu tribe are a very strong, self-sufficient people. It would be an honour for this group to use the Bantu name as a symbol of what they're striving for.' Dads always talked proper.

'Who would understand that?'

'Ah ha! Never underestimate the minds of humble people! I shall explain it to them and then put it to the vote.'

'They'll vote about the name?'

'Everybody has to have their say . . .'

'But you've already decided it!'

'Yes, Bantu People!' Yan started drumming on the table.

'The whole group will choose and elect their own leaders.'

'Bantu People coming to Tamarind Grove?'

'And where'll this happen anyway? All the weighing and distribution you were talking about?' Mums asked patiently.

'What? What it is they weighing and distributing?' Yan asked, turning to Dads. We all looked at Dads, then as he started talking, drifted off. I checked Sammy pushing around her food on her plate. Emanja was trying to focus on something over Dads's head.

'The Bantu Society will provide the people of Tamarind Grove with a source of income. Anyone can join, become a member and choose what and how much they want to process. As long as they do their share of some of the necessary chores.'

'Which are?'

'Weighing and recording the quantities.'

'But what it is dey weighing and giving out?' Yan asked again.

Dads shot him a look.

'The Guyana Marketing Co-op – the GMC – sells fresh ginger and cassava and there is an export market for *dried* ginger and starch.'

Dads went on with what the Bantus would do. He was gleaming again. My eyes shifted to Mums. Sometimes when everybody was talking, words flying back and forth, I played ping-pong with my eyes – seeing if I could keep up with the flying words. Big big townschool words from them big sisters. Some garbled-up ones from Yan's big mouth. Little short ones from Saskia. Curly quick ones from Sammy. Just kept batting them up and down the long table to the next player.

Mums's slow steady words bounced heavily down towards Dads. 'So this sorting and collecting will go on downstairs I guess?'

'Well, it is the biggest bottom-house around. And the only reason we live here is to help improve the village.

'Trucks coming and going.' Bounced down the table slower. Barely avoiding the dishes.

'That'll only be fortnightly!' Dads's words sprang back.

'People coming and going, in and out'a the yard. Making noise.'

'Oh, that wouldn't bother me!'

'OK. I don't want to hear you complaining when you can't get any peace and quiet.' The words rolled all the way to Dads. Going quietly round the glasses and the big jug. Coming to rest with a soft butt against the edge of Dads's plate.

In the crook of the house was the big fat Buxton Spice Mango Tree. So close-up to the house it could see everything: through the upstairs windows, the window on the landing, the kitchen, even into the bathroom and toilet. So big I couldn't climb it. Was one tree I didn't like. Walking down the stairs you could feel this thing knowing what you're thinking. Your head gets to level with the window and there's this thick, black and green arm, just there. It knew too much. All the bickerings in the kitchen, the whisperings in the bedrooms, even your private toilet-seat thoughts – a damn mango leaf always scratching on the outside of the frosted pane. Yowaris lived in it. And lichen and fungus and the big Powis bird. Ripe black-spotty mangoes splattered the concrete below. Sometimes Ramesh and Mikey would climb up for the firm bunches. Fooling around, showing off thirty feet above the septic tank. Foolishness. I watched them silently from my bedroom window. Pretending I didn't even want any green mangoes.

Late at night, my bigger sisters'd show off too. Going out on the roof in the moonlight to pick green mangoes. And eating them right there. Lolling off and behaving ridiculous.

Its mangoes were sweet but I never wanted it to know how much I enjoyed them. But the damn thing would know anyway. It knew everything and wouldn't tell me nuthing. Just there, swelling-up itself with all the secrets. Not just our house secrets. It could see all of the street in front our house. Into the Peters's house across the other side, on to the roof of the shed opposite us, to the DeAbros' shop. Even inside Aunt Ruth's closed-up house behind the shop. And into Miss Isaac's cow pen. Into all the side streets, and through the windows of the Pastor's house. On Saturdays it watched all the market stalls setting up, unfolding and spreading from Mainroad to Teacher Dolly's yard. It could see the games children were playing in the schoolyard, could see the gas station where Bottom House Crappo sat at night. Past Mainroad – quite over so – down Backdam. Could even see the fruits on the trees and the sharp green shine of the water-hyacinth leaves clogging the brown canals down there.

All around too. It could see behind our house. Behind the empty lot to the hot, still cemetery. Knew where Mr Man was buried and where Pasa the gravedigger would dig the next grave. And on to where the red-mud banks of the big Broadie Canal was smooth from us sliding down into the milky-tea water. Saw us splashing and pushing each other into the deep part, where we not supposed to swim.

Could even see over the roofs, between the tall swaying coconut trees, past the dome of the broken mosque, to the endless seawall and the distant brown sea. It could see when the tide went out and fishermen on wooden planks crouched and kicked their way out, sliding to their seines staked in the mud. Fast snails slithering out on miles of smooth grey mud, leaving glistening sunset trails. Returning sluggishly, boxes loaded with flopping fish, thick mud socks up to their knees and veins pumping on their thighs.

I knew it could hear things going on everywhere in Guyana. Sounds that went on in Berbice Mad House, New Amsterdam Town Hall, the President's House in Georgetown, Linden Bauxite Workers Union. It could hear the sugar cane being crushed through the big iron rollers in Enmore Estate. And even catch the sweet husky paddy smell from the rice mill in Mahaicony. All these things and more. All the horrible dark-road secrets, the plotting and scheming. But it wouldn't tell me things.

Between the piano room and the soya room was the school room. When all the windows lock up, is pitch black inside there except for one beam of light from a round hole in the wall under the sink. Plenty things gone through that room. Was classroom, store room, playroom for Husband and Wife. That was the room where Sexy Marilyn get screw. Is true too. Must have been rape but she was wanting it. She was only laughing all through and looking real rosy afterwards. We heard everything. Couldn't see everything – only through that one hole smelling of concrete. All them boys and Marilyn in there in that pitch black. We could hear them touching. And they knew we outside craning. Sexy Marilyn laughing in a adult way. The DeAbro boys – Iggy, Manny, Bernard – and my brother Yan, hustling round her. They couldn't see shit in there either. Just feeling around on Marilyn. Clumsy stupidy boys. Their laughs and whisperings sounding more girlie than Marilyn's.

31

The peep-hole shaft of light fell on the leg of the long table. Peeping sideways, you could just see the hem of Marilyn's skirt and a piece of her leg dangling. It shaking and hitting the magazines on the shelf underneath. She must'a been sitting on top that weak tabletop, shaking up the whole thing. Couldn't see no sign of her other leg. Then one of them boys' jeans would block the hole or a short-pants one would lean up by the table leg – hand on crotch, squeezing it. When Iggy passed through the light, his red running shorts had a bigger bump in front than his big batty bumping out behind.

Her bubbies must'a been out too but she didn't have her clothes off. We knew she had longish round-end bubbies and a big-woman body. Only a couple years older than Judy but her bubbies was already ripe. Judy's mother say 'too much man pull them.' That's what does happen when you let man start touching them too early – they grow fast. So now, all big-bubbie girls look like they take plenty man. Marilyn like to take man. And she takes big man too. She had a big man from Nabaclis who used to give she all kinds of clothes and gold bracelets. Pretty girl, like she. Red oiled skin and a laughy face with nice teeth and dimples. Used to do her hair in little-girl ringlets. Soon as she see a boy or a man, she start smiling, laughing. What the big man and them call *ir-re-sist-ible*. She used to sit next to me in the mixed class in that same middle room, until we had a fight. She stabbed me in the arm with her lead pencil and the point broke in my skin. That stopped me – couldn't believe she would hurt me so bad. Stabbed me with her left hand, same left hand she would write her curly writing with. But didn't have the sense to write the correct answers.

Sexy Marilyn lived down Sideline with her mother. And

her mother always quarrelling with her, chase her out the house plenty times for taking man. Though the mother used to take it too – that's where Marilyn must'a got a taste for it. She throw way baby already too. Marilyn is problems. And them stupidy boys inside there was no match for her. While she sounding like it nice, they fighting up. Grunting and panicking, grabbing with sweaty hands. Didn't even know bout sucking her bubbies. She must'a told them to but they didn't do it. Listening to them after . . . they thought she was trying to trick them into doing stupidness. All a'them got it except Manny. Iggy most of all. He be the one shaking up the table so much. Every now and then one of them would *steups* and slap the peeping hole, sending concrete grains straight in your eye. Wished I could just buss open them windows and see just how they was doing it. And they was taking so long! They didn't care bout Ramesh looking out for them by the back step. Hear they do she from behind too. That was when the leg moved and you couldn't see no skin but the table was jerking hard. She liked it too. Was plenty commotion then. Soon after that, they done. Like she had to go. And she swanned out of the front gate sexier than ever. Wet patches under her arms and glowing from every pore. Iggy, Manny, Bernard and Yan stumbled out, rubbing their eyes and blinking, itchy, agitated. We pushed past them into the room. Hurried in hoping to find *e-vi-dence*, something left to show us. But in the darkness all we found was a warm human smell. A moist rich smell. Until we slammed open the windows and let in the light.

After that I looked at Iggy harder. I knew he used to screw girls but now I could smell it on him. I didn't like him really. Was almost afraid of him. He had a beasty-human way bout everything. When he peed against the zinc sheets of the pig pens, you could hear it a mile away. He had rider's teeth and snored loud. Even when he breathed normal was a rasping sound. He'd lick his lips and rub his tongue on his teeth and stick it out at me, then wink.

Ignatius DeAbro was trouble. One of the fourteen children in the Portuguese family next door, he was football player and pig pen cleaner. We'd shout out 'Iggy Piggy, pig in the pen. Fart pon pig an clean pig pen!' He'd shake the living daylights out'a you or beat his sisters with the back of his hand. But now he was being unusually kind to me. He must'a realized that I was looking at him different. I noticed the rubbing slapping movement where his thighs overlapped and pulled his shorts up in a bunch. His white skin always wet on his legs under all that black hair. And the curls on his head bouncing in all different directions, sometimes with bits of bran from the pig food barrel stuck in them.

I watched him from the upstairs window waddling down the road from football, ball in a net rolling on his back. Calves in muddy socks shaking every time his pegged shoe hit the asphalt. And he always cheerful, confident, as if he never had anything to do with spading pig shit. He would wrestle a pig to the ground and smash in its head with a hammer every Friday. Then when he finished gutting and cleaning it, scrubbed pink-clean and smelling of Sunlight soap, he'd sit down and eat a mountain of rice. Slap his stomach, belch, lean back and pick his teeth. Fine T'ings he called me, cause I was skinny. He liked thick girls. I saw him slap Mrs Peters's huge arse once. She turned round and gave him one back. As he got bigger, older women looked at him more and he'd call out to them in a familiar way on the street.

This day, he blocked me by the small fridge in the school room. It was late afternoon and somebody'd already closed some of the windows. The air was reddish, a rectangle of weak rosy light shone through from the soya room next door. I pressed into the corner by the fridge and closed window. Iggy wasn't touching me, just leaning on the fridge and windowsill, close up, breathing on me.

'Whey you going, eh?' His mouth laughing but his eyes strange.

I scared stiff or excited, must be what the word *fri-gid* means – frozen, your heart beating up inside and legs quivering, all freeze-up. While I frigid like that, he came right up on to me, pressing me into the jutting windowsill. His warm breath pushed my hair away and smelt sweet-bran and brackish. His earlobes turned bright red as he pressed the hardest piece of flesh against my burning, shivering bunge. Right hard against my bone. The brute was surprised by the big hard mound I had too, made him look down to where the heat was coming from. But it made him bore his hard lolo on me more, and he gripped the top of my arm with one hand, his fingers overlapping. My matchbox dress, taught across my thighs, stopped him wedging his leg in between them. Hot air from the fridge blew up my legs to my crotch. His other hand pushed up and grabbed my clammy panty. Same time, the twitching in my bunge made one big blink and I felt a warm liquid wet his fingers.

'Lula. Dinner time' came from the kitchen upstairs.

His breathing checked a little, his palm slipping on my arm now and neck dripping with sweat. Breath puffing down the front of my dress where my smell was coming up from. Coarse hair bushing up in my face.

'You lucky,' he muttered, pulling his hand out of my pee-soaked panty and squeezing his lolo so hard I thought it'd break.

To the side of the bulge he was squeezing was a wet patch. Made me check my dress front. Dry. The skin on my thighs tingled.

'Lula!'

'Coming now.'

Worrying how I was going to sit down with this soaked panty-crotch, I was still quaking-frigid. All my mauve dress jumping over my heart. Looking at him, chewing my lip and squeezing my legs to stop the trembling. But didn't want the feeling to stop. Felt brazen now but weak and kind of sorry for Iggy squeezing his cock in front of me, snorting with his head down.

Next to the Buxton Spice, above the round wooden vat and straddling the paling, was the Sweet Genip Tree. A tall, spread-out, fine leaf tree. Very fruitful too. In genip season, bucketfuls of sweet-sweet genips were part of our school mornings and sitting-reading afternoons. Cracking the skin with your teeth and slipping the seed into your mouth, sucking the juice at the same time, then flinging the skin into another bucket became a mechanical movement. If you got into the rhythm good, you could slip in a fresh one and put the old seed back into the new skin without messing up your hands. Sometimes the same seed would stay in my mouth for hours, it went from juicy, lychee-like flesh to wet cotton wool, till my tongue rolled all the little burrs off the seed.

Was a nice light feeling up in this Sweet Genip Tree. It made you forget about the sweet genips hanging all around on the ends of the branches. Swaying breeze ran leopard-spot shadows over your leg. You forgot too about the sharp paling underneath. Level with the fretwork of Teacher Dolly's roof, you could look down and see the dull gleam of her bedroom floor through the open jalousie shutters. Miss Elsie and Miss Myrtle used to sleep in that room. The two of them was spinsters. The real meaning of that word. Just had to look at them and know. Spindly and rigid, old virgins, petticoats and long cotton drawers. They were Teacher Dolly's cousins and lived further up the road. But every evening at six they'd come over to Teacher Dolly with their bundles and sleep the night to keep each other company. They had to look out for one another. Teacher Dolly was older than the other two, in her eighties. She had been the more educated, richer, free-up cousin, was even engaged once. Her house was grander than theirs and appearances had to be kept up. The tall, tight-lipped, high-coloured cousins helped her while still struggling to keep their dignity and their own house in order. Now Elsie was dead. And the younger, quieter Myrtle seemed to shake a little more when she walked down the road with her bundle at six o'clock. Lounging around in the frangipani tree just inside Teacher Dolly's front gate, the four of a'we girls would greet her.

The couple of paling staves missing from the fence between Teacher Dolly's yard and ours expanded our world of trees. Teacher Dolly's Sapodillas was the sweetest ones. They ringed her house and made her backyard a dense, dark green, sticky-sap cave. Her dungs tree was special too. Big, huge dungs and never enough of them. Teacher Dolly's Dungs Tree was her joy and pain. Every day schoolchildren bricked and pelted them down, pretending they couldn't hear Teacher Dolly screeching and banging her windowsill. Somehow she managed to save some of them big juicy dungs and displayed them in a crystal bowl on her pristine mahogany dining table, a centrepiece on a stiff white doily. She said they was her 'apples' and would offer them to us. Those ones always tasted better than the ones we had just t'iefed downstairs.

Most afternoons, Teacher Dolly'd just be in her rocking chair in the front gallery. Rocking and looking out. The lady that came in every day to clean and cook would be gone, leaving Teacher Dolly all freshly bathed and powdered, silver hair combed rippling past her temples, hands clasped gently in her lap. The sagging skin on her arms so soft and light to touch. I'd sit with her sometimes, she rocking and me drapsing myself on the hard chaise-longue next to her. In that still, shiny front gallery, with Teacher Dolly rocking and the breeze blowing the sapodilla trees outside, nothing could ever change. Except me. I'd be the only thing changing. Growing, right there on that chaise-longue. The granny sugar that fell to the ground from the termites' hole in the windowsill would fall the same way tomorrow. The delicate fern in the brass pot on the skinny table next to me would be the same too. The gramophone box, the bent cane chairs and sideboard. But I was young and strong and growing in that front gallery. Sitting there growing while Teacher Dolly rocked. The chairs filled up with the people we imagined. Dressed-up people. Me dressed up and grown up too, and dancing. I danced around on that shiny floor to the music of the gramophone, my feet small in soft white shoes, my waist perfect, petticoats sticking out the skirt of my yellow cotton dress. My bust is small and neat and I'm tall, erect. And the most graceful dancer of all these ladies, swirling with the tallest, handsomest gentleman of course. I can't even tell you how handsome he is but he's making me fly and spin. Teacher Dolly's eyes'd sparkle, she's so happy for me because my beau is a bit like her Godfrey and she'd be remembering her days and the stories she told me. Miss Elsie'd be serving clinking glasses of fresh lemonade with ice and Miss Myrtle offered tiny cheese and cucumber sandwiches. Until it was six o'clock. Then the real Miss Myrtle came through the front gate and across the front yard with her bundle. She'd come up the back steps through the empty rooms, past the closed-up gramophone, and take up her seat in one of the cane chairs near the front door, cracking it open so she could see out.

'Good-night Teacher Dolly, have a nice evening, sleep well. Good-evening, Miss Myrtle, I going now.'

'Good-night blessed child. God bless you. Say hello to Mums and Dads.'

I went home every time feeling young and blessed indeed and tomorrow when I went back, they and their world would be the same. I'd be two inches taller.

TWO

Up by the seawall was the ruins of an old mosque. Wasn't ancient ruins, just a few years old, looked like it was half built and then something had bumped into it. Glass shards and goat poop trailed through the roofless rooms. Grass grew on the walls and water collected in the holes. Mums said it was Riots made it so. Race Riots before we moved in. Fires and bombs chasing Indians out. Now Tamarind Grove was black race people, strong PNC party people. Dads, Bunty family and Aunty Babe was the only East Indians. And my family was mixed – Indian, black and white. Bunty was a butcher – beef at that. He wasn't like the other Hindus who settled around the sugar estates since the days of their great-grandparents. People said he didn't want to cut cane or plant garden. And he had no money to set up a shop, couldn't even buy a cow. When he moved to Tamarind Grove, he came with two small pigs and a grim face. Aunty Babe was the only other Indian left in Tamarind Grove – a squingy old lady breeze could knock down.

Black people lived in one village, Indians the next. Blacks, Indians. So it went, all along the coast of Guyana to Mahaica. Even if you didn't see people, you could tell which village was black, which was coolie. Black villages had co-op shops; Indians hardware and dry goods. Blacks had un-painted houses and clap-hand churches; Indians paint, front gardens, mosques and temples. Was always people liming on the road in a black village. Mothers and children out till ten at night. Not so in an Indian village. But all had Catholic churches and rumshops by the main road.

Was difficult to imagine this broken mosque full of Indians praying and living in Tamarind Grove. Seemed to me, the only way a building could get like this was like in war movies when they just dropped those bombs whistling, straight down from planes. Them Riots must'a been like that. The only warring I could remember was what Mums said was a rally. I remember plenty PNC people running down the street with flames in bottles. And even though they were shouting, faces orange, teeth gold – was a strange silence in the black night. That silence made my parents say nothing. Close the windows and hold us. Hearts galloping.

I went to church in a mosque once, you know, with Dads and Mr Mohammed. In town. He lived in East Riumvelt and we used to buy Volkswagen parts from him. Don't know what he doing in that area, the Indian section of town was more by the East Bank side. Home upstairs, shop downstairs. He had to unlock two padlocks to let you in. Dark musty room crowded with black car parts, greasy receipt books and the smell of engine oil. Mr Mohammed quoted the price, gold teeth flashing, always freshly shaved, white shirt spanning his fat arms and belt dividing his jelly stomach in half. While his eldest son punished behind the counter, wafer thin, never could do anything right. We followed Mr Mohammed's wide bottom up a choky stairway. His pants was bloated with goady – swell-up testicles hanging halfway down his leg. At the top, blowing hard, he introduced his wife. She gracefully avoided shaking anybody's hand and led us through the dining room, where the youngest son sat at the plastic-covered table doing homework.

Mrs Mohammed had a charm that made up for her husband's lack of it, moving easily about the crowded living room with its photos of children overseas. She seated Mr Mohammed in a worn leather chair, us on the red furry settee and had us drinking soft drinks in no time. She wasn't shy at all but hid behind huge glasses that were just dark enough so you couldn't see her eyes. She prattled on bout her big children in Canada and, through things she didn't say, let you know that there had been better days. The half-scrubbed-off flowers on the drinking glass and her lack of jewellery told you so too.

'My son in the dining room is very bright. He only like to keep his head in the books.'

Her unmentioned daughter appeared with some sweetmeats. Daddy's little pet, eyes and hair flashing. Small hands held the red lacquered tray and her feet were clean and soundless.

A glass bottle full of fire had been thrown into their living room. Pieces of glass flew in Mrs Mohammed's face, one piece in her eye. Now wire meshing covered the windows from the sills to the edge of the roof. Mr Mohammed said even the roof was burglar-proofed, and not a black man would mess with him again.

'In this neighbourhood everybody owe me.'

Was Mr Mohammed's mosque I went to with my father for some special service. Was busy looking to sing like how you do in a temple. Was nervous all the way through cause I didn't know what to do. I knew I had to keep my head covered and look down but wanted to see what was going on. They didn't even have fancy altars or gods to look at, just a boring chant that went on for hours before the feasting began. After the service, all the white gowns billowed in the yard blending with curry, black outlined eyes, sandalled feet and sweetmeats. Children ran bursting through the clouds of fabric. The men spoke with deep voices trapped in beards and their heads were crocheted studs, holding down the billows.

We the only service now in this broken mosque. Windswept steps standing on their own, bits of blue and white tile scattered between the round columns. Closed my eyes, clasped my hands and Judy blessed me from the top step. I walked down under the dome and knelt and bent forward, arms out straight. Allah'd up and down, up and down like I'd seen, mumbling in my beard.

'**B** uss he fucking head.'
'Walk, you dog you. You walking to reach de station.'
'Get up, you scunt you. Walk!'

The beds in the house spat everybody out. Straight to the front windows. I got a window to myself and crouched at it, bridge of my nose against the sill, adjusting my eyes to the dark outside. Blows falling like rain on something I couldn't see. Greenheart staves thudding on flesh and bone. Loud above the shouts from men's bellies and the women's screams. Women flying out from pale homes in the moonlight. Tearing paling staves out of their fences. Nylon nighties ripping, skin gleaming, bare feet thrashing through drains and knees grating on gravel to get at the thing. Miss Harper bawling. Stamping and shaking all over, holding her head with a couple curlers hanging off.

'All! All!' spurred her sister, plunging through the backs of men dragging and beating the thing. 'Kill him!'

Somebody grabbed her from the back by her duster and it ripped open, bubbies flopping out. An arm around her neck and a handful of hair stopped her clawing and charging. A twang of a broadside cutlass rang clear. More thuds and whutucks rained.

'Walk, you fucking dog.'

A leg black with blood flashed through the crowd.

'You go learn.'

A paling point rammed through the thick bodies and stopped dead on bone. The bent backs dipped down and pulled up a head and an arm that dangled a wet hand from somewhere between the elbow and wrist. It flopped about for a minute or so, carried slowly forward before dropping back into the writhing caterpillar of bodies.

I heard Dads's muted voice on the telephone urging the police. Someone was pulling the back of my shirt. I clung to the windowframe, pressing my forehead hard against the bumpy frosted pane. My eyes followed the twisting mass crawling down the street. More women and children flying out of streets and darkness. Some joining the men, some heading in the opposite direction towards Miss Harper's house.

Mr Harper must'a been at work. He was a security guard at Enmore Estate. If he had ketch them, they'd be done. Was two a'them t'iefing. One got away up by the seawall. This one was hiding in the sugarcane clump by Harper's back step. He uncorked the septic tank and climbed in. Didn't shut it back properly and people heard the swishing inside. He been drowning in the shit mixture, they poking him back under with the end of a rake, swallowing the stuff till he was hooked out. The hands that grabbed him didn't mind the stench, gave blows that sent shit flying and blood pouring. They mash-up both legs by the time he reach Mainroad. Now everything must be broken, crushed. One man had a metal pipe – made a hollow sound when he stamped it on the road.

'Stand up! Walk!'

No human sound came from the centre of the squirming caterpillar. Just dull thuds. The sound of shoes hitting stomach.

Three policemen came half trotting down the road.

'Leggo, leggo, leggo! Loose de man.'

As they neared the mass, batons out, the flesh and legs of the caterpillar fell away and the guts lay bare. The purple-black twitching pile glistened.

'Oh shit! He stink! He stinking man, he stink!'

They dragged him to Cove & John Police Station, entrails of bloodied nighties and sweating bodies following. The dents on my forehead from the patterned glass slowly filled back out.

News came buzzing down the road into the yard, straight to us under the Sweet Dungs Tree. It didn't even have time to go through Sammy, Miss Guyana Broadcasting Corporation. It just flew from the seawall to here. We pelt out'a the yard and up the road before it had time to reach the big people upstairs. Speeding up the road, our soles barely touching the mid-morning-warm asphalt. Slowed down reaching the gravel road to Scheme. Then under foot was soft dirt and grass. Bounced the one-plank bridge over Forty Canal fast as the springing board let us, eyes open wide and breath held, trying to match the rhythm of the last person without looking down.

A small crowd gathered on the Koker bridge over Fifty Canal and a fearful sort of anticipation made us start walking towards them. Slowed down even more as we got closer. Now the rank smell of sea mud and dead seaweed pushed up in your face. On the bridge, the warm-tar smell of the big black Koker sluice took over. Right up close, I could see bubbles in the thick tar. Pressed my finger on it, left a soft dent. Couldn't hear what people was saying. My ears ringing. Something was out there in the mud.

Every day at low tide the Koker's doors opened and muddy fresh water, lilies, water grass, dead dogs and whatever else gushed from the canals to meet the sea a mile or so out. The rush of water cut a deep wet gash in the mudflats defined by sloping stone walls and big barnacle-covered piles that stuck up, gappy. Crooked teeth in smooth mud gums.

People were buzzing around on the bridge, then pushing round the huge concrete base, round the rusty pegged sluice wheel wound with rusty cables. Flowing like ants, down along the top of the stone wall and on to the mud. Wasn't many other children around. We followed the line of people struggling, some up to their thighs in the mud. The line turned sharply around something lying there. Then snaked back, scattering people to the seawall. The brackish, sea-rank stench stuck in my throat as I sank. I sucked my feet in and out of mud lips. The only thing to do was to keep going. Sucking, pushing, pulling. We held hands instinctively, the four a'we, struggling forward, mouths gummed up, blood screaming. A face. The Pastor's wife. It was her face. Dead. Half in the mud, mouth open, stuffed with muddy grass. Her bare body twisted, just a piece of red shirt on one shoulder. Dull black skin in the sun. A gash on her neck glinted and between her legs more grass stuck out that had been stuffed into her bunge. Some water swirled against her stomach and arm, then down into the holes of mud holding my feet.

*

51

'Who would do such a t'ing, eh, Rose?' Mrs DeAbro was saying to Mums. 'Ah mean, is de Pastor wife! What dis place coming to, eh? You could tell me dat? Is murder we reach? Is not just rape, is kill. Dey had to kill she too? Lord!

'I would'a never believe dis could happen in Tamarind Grove. Times changing, Mums, I telling you. You watch an see. When dem Army fellars behaving so lawless round de place, and de government encouraging it – what you expect?

'I hear is some young boys from Scheme dat do it. Four a'dem. She was taking a short cut through de ball field, and dey hold she there. Five o'clock in de morning, Mums. I does be up dat time in de morning too. Rape! De woman was coming from she mudda house. Moving stuff to dey new house here.

'De Pastor wife, Mums. An dey have three young chi'ren. All my married life I living here, Rose, thirty-six years. Nothin like dis eva happen. I don' know what t'ings coming to, Lord. I really don' know.'

I sat on the toilet seat. The mango-leaf pattern shifted and swayed on the windowpane. But I wasn't going to look at it. The Buxton Spice leaves rustled. I still didn't look round. Fixed my eyes on the putty between the wooden planks of the wall in front of me. The thick old leafy hand of the tree scraped and scratched the glass.

'What you bothering me for? You can't see I thinking?'

One of its big body-branches creaked outside the window.

'I can't talk now, I thinking. And anyway you don' even tell me nuthing . . . even when you watched them fellars *rape* de Pastor wife! Even though it was still dark, you must'a seen something! You see *everyt'ing*. You must'a heard a noise. She didn't make noise? You ever see rape before? You know all bout dat an you don' tell me nuthing. So what you troubling me for?'

The leaves swayed again outside and the pattern danced across the window. I opened the window and propped it up with the spare toilet-paper roll. Through the gap, the breeze and bits of leaves and the breath of the Buxton Spice wafted in. It rested its arm on the slanted pane and bent and peered in at me.

'Why you don' tell me nuthing? Bout how come people come to have murder. And riots. Race Riots. You know bout dat. You know dat Burnham cause dat. You must know he well – Our Leader Comrade Linden Forbes Burnham. Yes. He have bug-eye just like you. And he always hearing everyt'ing like you. Mums tell me dat he cause de Race Riots. He make black people hate Indians. He take everyt'ing de Indians had an say is government own. He put big fat black people to run de sugar an rice factories. You must'e see all dat. You is a black Buxton Spice or what?

'If you know so much, how come, we is part coolie an we living in Tamarind Grove? And DeAbros is Putagee, an dey living here too?

'Dat's why Powis does poop on you – you too stingy. Knowing all dem things an just there holding it in. That's what make you swell-up eh? Make you grow so big-up? And you still spreading out yourself, curling out new hands and leaves. You must'e suck in everything and swallow it already.'

I leant forward and looked through the window gap, down to the root of the tree. The fat knobbly feet were cracking up the concrete, bending the water pipe, reaching under the vat. Only left for them to crack the septic tank. I sat back and a big breeze ruffled the whole top of the Buxton Spice, a distant leaf-surf sound rippling overhead. Level with my window slot, the twisted body groaned and swayed lazily. The arm resting on the window barely moved.

THREE

Emelda married Ricardo DeAbro at sixteen and had eighteen children, fourteen of them still living. Judy and Rachel were the last. In her fifties now, Mrs DeAbro had a head of short salt 'n' pepper hair, spectacles – a recent addition – and a worried look most of the time. Tallish and trim, she was proud of her figure for her age.

'Is just the high belly . . . is from the chi'ren you know, and is the pressure killing me Mums.'

Many times she'd say to my mother 'Dese chi'ren will kill me, Rose. When I drop down one'a dese days, God alone know what dey will do, them same ones that killing me.'

The skin on her arms and face was weathered, brownish and thick with little creases criss-crossing, but the skin on her back and thighs was smooth and white. When her big girls forced her to rest, she'd have the four a'we pamper her by plucking out her grey 'biting' hairs till she fell asleep. Or scrape the dandruff on her scalp with a fine-teeth comb. Or sap Limacol on her back and neck. We'd sit on the front steps, her shoulders between Rachel's knees, and while we singled out the biting hairs, she'd swiggle the tip of a fowl feather in her ear and close her eyes. The clack of her false teeth as her jaw dropped open would tell us she was asleep. If you moved or pulled a healthy black hair by mistake, she'd wake back up and ask why you stopped. Always crotchety, she ruled the DeAbro household. She barely managed to make ends meet, yet still she felt a little above the rest of the women of Tamarind Grove.

She and Ricardo built the house from scratch. He was a carpenter and a fisherman then moved up to shopkeeping. As the children came they extended their house. Started keeping pigs downstairs, bought a piece of land on the roadside and set up the first shop in this side of the village. Everybody came to buy basics: bread, rice, sugar, milk, sanitary napkins and salt. Theirs was not the only big-size family, not the richest or most educated, so must'a been because they was Portuguese that Mrs DeAbro felt above 'de commoners'. That and having connections with people from Away. She wasn't arrogant though. She slaved away to keep things going and, because of that, the other women didn't scorn her. They just kept their distance. She often said, half woeful, that she and Ricardo wouldn't even dream of living anywhere else. This is what they had worked for.

Ricardo was pink and meticulous. When he was sober he had a slow solid way of moving and hardly spoke in the house. Slept in the shop. His clothes had to match. He combed his curls forward, set them with Mohini Hair Oil and water. Blotches on the face had to be covered with Mrs DeAbro's base-powder. Newspaper folded and put in back pockets, for his bumsey to look firm. Tucking in the shirt, zipping up and buckling his belt he left till he reached on to the street and was walking across to the shop.

All the Portuguese families in Guyana was related: Fernandez, Rodriguez, Gomes, DaSilva, Deguiar, DaCosta, DeAbro and others. Some of them got rich – rum distillers, wholesalers or 'pork knockers' dredging gold. But they were still 'Putagee', not even local whites. Seemed like all pure Putagee families had their simple one. Theodore was the DeAbros' cross. Theo, or 'Brother Boots', stayed home even though he was in his thirties. He got married once. To a tall Putagee girl named Norma. Nobody could figure out how she ended up with him. Nobody asked questions. After a grand wedding with Norma towering above all the men, dancing in her white lace gown, they went off in a car, gone on honeymoon. A few months later, Theo returned home in a donkey cart with all his new clothes and furniture. Nobody asked him nuthing.

Theo looked after the pigs, a vital role in the family. Because of this, he commanded a certain respect that you could feel bristling around him. He loved the pigs. Looked after them better than anyone could. Patted them, slapped them, talked a language with them. Even when he slaughtered them to fill the wooden barrels in the shop with salt pork, he did it in a way you couldn't question. He had long brown hair, dead straight and greasy, a grisly beard and small quick eyes you hardly ever saw. Hunched over, small-built and stringy, his real skin colour only came through when he'd go out to drink with 'de Boys'. He'd scrub then. But usually he was dark and grimy from the slaughtering and from carrying pig halves on his back across the road to the shop. Or from fetching pig feed in from the road, fetching coal bags or cleaning pig pens. He didn't look or feel comfortable in anything new or clean for very long but would cuss violently and fight, beat the pigs and loose-out his sheep, if anyone borrowed his ninety-dollar 'new-brand' hat. And then go back into himself, growling deeply, rolling all the words and cusses together. When he was being friendly, he'd just 'oouts' and grabbed at us, made us jump and squeal like his piglets when he teased them like that. After a drinking session, he'd come home and curl up among the pigs or in the coals box. Sometimes they'd find him under the wooden settee on the verandah where the dog slept.

He was Mrs DeAbro's embarrassment but her pet. When the boys teased him, she defended him. She gave him his space in their small house and was always reminding us that Theo was a big man. She'd always keep a good piece of meat for him or hide his portion of stew from the others. His affection for her came out daily in the tasks he silently took upon himself to do: cleaning out her chicken coop, collecting the eggs, cleaning the drains. Often her gratitude came wailing out, she'd screech and sob that if it wasn't for Theo she'd be breaking her back and nobody would notice. Nobody!

'Iggy, Manny, Ber . . . nard!' Mrs DeAbro was always bawling after the boys. Making herself hoarse. 'Iggy, Manny, Ber . . . nard!'

Bernard was the eldest of the three last boys of the family, was Anne-Marie's twin. He slept in the shop with Ricardo and was already a wiry toughened man-boy, kept to himself and had just started gambling. Iggy was the one that gave Emelda back-chat and blood pressure. And Emanuel, or Manny, the youngest, was put aside to study. Felix, her favourite, was gone already, he was the first one to reach Away. Before he went to Canada, he used to live and work in town. He helped the family acquire their prized possession, the Gramophone. The big wooden tapered box had radio knobs and gilded mesh covering the speakers set in the front. The top lifted up, with the turntable and record rack deep down inside. It was covered with a varnished tan veneer, and stood proudly on spindly legs. After gramophones and jukeboxes went out and black stereos with big speakers, chromed knobs and jumping dials came in, the Gram became a sideboard for doilies, crocheted swans and porcelain dogs. Felix was the one who knew about music other than Jim Reeves and Patsy Cline. He played endless Bee Gee LPs. Them big girls got even more up to date, asked him to bring John Travolta's hits. We'd do the moves, shaking up the cabinet. Since he went to Canada, he married a Canadian lady and sent Mrs DeAbro studio photos of the first overseas grandchild. She put them on the old Gram with the ones of the new Canada in-laws.

The drawing room was divided into two by different types of furniture. The back drawing room only had wrought-iron chairs with flower-patterned plastic seats. The front drawing room had the suite, and was put aside for visitors and holidays. Was the older girls' display of pride and taste and Mrs DeAbro's satisfaction in life. Most times, we wasn't even allowed to pass through it to reach the verandah. Anne-Marie and Agnes, the two older girls still at home, reupholstered the suite with orange furry fabric. They chose the orange synthetic lace curtains for the front windows too, changing them at Christmas time for red ones in the centre with two white ones at the ends like they'd seen in the McCalls magazines. One Christmas, they bought a piece of chocolate-brown carpet for the area, allowed us to walk on it after bathing, to sit and feel with our toes how soft and thick it was, before banning us till Christmas Day. Thought it was luxury.

Agnes was older than Anne-Marie, was in charge of the cooking and helped with decisions. But it was Anne-Marie's job to keep the front drawing room looking like a display. She had a steady routine. Brush the blue tentesse wall, wipe the crucifix and wall plaque, every surface. Then kneel down and ruffle and smooth the carpet pile while backing out on to the lino strip that ran from the kitchen through to the front door. Every Friday she'd take out the carpet and beat it over the verandah wall. Then polish the whole floor, buffing it to a deep rich shine, always ending up on the lino strip. Was the only time I'd see her sweat, with her big bubbies jiggling around vigorously and short pants digging into the front of her thighs. By the time she finished, she'd be all red in the face, pimples alive, shirt-front wet, red marks on her thighs, and knees black. But she'd be happy. Until someone stepped off the lino and on to her floor.

Later when Anne-Marie went to live in town, it became Judy's job but it was never the same unless Mrs DeAbro harassed all morning to get it done properly. Eventually Judy and Rachel convinced Mrs DeAbro to varnish the whole floor, to keep up with the times and to save them from having black knees like Anne-Marie.

Mrs DeAbro could never understand why we didn't have a front drawing room. We had a 'living room'. She said was cause my parents had lived abroad for so long. On the big wooden floor of our living room, we had the Tibisiri straw mat. Our armchairs had cotton covers. Patterned calabashes, strange carvings and paintings, made it more obeah-like to superstitious Emelda. She kept telling Mums that the calabashes going to stop us getting money.

'And why Mums don't want curtain on de windows? Or buy carpet and ornaments, dese t'ings dat give a woman so much pride? Education, dat's what happen to them. Too much. Look at all dem books dey have in de place. Everywhere you look is jus books. And look at how you father does keep himself! He can't wear a proper shoe instead'a dem flip-flaps? And cut off dat long beard he have on he face? Youall have money – he always travelling overseas – why Dads go an buy a bruk-down old van so?

'And broughtupsy – youall does eat with knife and fork every day. Set up the table fancy with all kind'a napkin an t'ing. Good-good manners. Good broughtupsy. Look how much white people youall know. An Ministers an all. Why it is youall mixing wid dem long-hair local people, eh? Have Rasta an' all sid down in de house. If Dads continue so, he going get youall in trouble. You t'ink I don' know dat a lot a'dem funny-looking people visiting youall is dem opposition people?

'You see me? Sitting right here on dis front step? I ain saying nuttin. Mums and Dads should know wha happening in dis place. I ain saying nuttin. Watch wha happening in de country – I don' understand it nuh! People can't even say boo in dey house – dey hearing it all de way in Parliament.

'T'ings not like long-time no more. People can't even watch out for each other no more yuh know. Cause by de time you turn round . . . is dem same ones juking you in yuh back. Like dem people in de Co-op.

'You see me? I sees nuttin. I hears nuttin. When dey ask me – I don't know what does go on by youall. I don' know nuttin nuh. I knows nuttin.'

She wanted her children educated – but not to end up like us.

Bullet, Sugar Baby and Rumshop Cockroach was the three whores of Tamarind Grove. They supported each other fiercely when they had to and bitched at each other in between. A sweet cool afternoon was just right to watch Sugar Baby slip-slapsing down the road in her cut-off jeans shorts, freshly bathed and powdered, no make-up on and a big comb stuck in her hair. She walked with untouchable attitude, braced back, one arm permanently akimbo, rolling on bow legs. Her high stomach led the way, popping open the top button of her shorts. In the heat of the day, her vest'd be pulled up and tucked under the flaps of her bubbies, showing more of the smooth red skin. Flat arse didn't matter in her case, she could get a man anyway. And the look on her face didn't matter either – mashed mouth with her bottom lip half-inch longer than the top one, chin jutting out under that. You gave her room when she came down the street and, with her head raked back, she just glanced through half-open slits, ready to steups at the slightest thing. She looked straight through children like they didn't exist, even though her belly high from having so many. Women got a cut-eye glance or a steups if they were young and dressed up stupid. Older women, whose husbands didn't fuck around, got a nod. She always added something to the rich languor of the afternoon that even I could recognize, my eyes following her slowly from the upstairs window. Something that held an edge of the night.

She was going to meet Bottom House Crappo who sold black pudding by Mainroad junction, spread there for the evening on a plastic bucket. Sugar Baby squatted between her huge knees, legs folded back on each other and wide open, showing the black parts of her inner thighs. Bottom House Crappo would comb Sugar's hair and by the time they done, the fluorescent gas-station lights and the street-lights would come on. If the night was busy enough, Sugar Baby'd go home to change and come back out. If it was quiet, she'd lime with Crappo till all the black pudding sold and then help her carry home her buckets and tray.

Sugar Baby's name used to be Baby Doll, before she get ketch. She didn't really get ketch though, was Mr DeAbro that get ketch. She and Bullet had a way they would go and lime on DeAbro's shop verandah. Liming and bustin big laugh. Laughing and bending down and slapping the wooden railing, bracing up on the stack of narrow doors that closed the shopfront. Whenever Mrs DeAbro came across to the shop, they'd waltz off. She would keep her silence until she got back home, then complain bout her tribulations. She always knew that Ricardo had a reason for not chasing them away from there.

That afternoon, Emelda DeAbro was blue already. It was before Felix had gone Away. Felix, her hope and dream, just gone and bought a second-hand car instead of saving up the money to go Canada. How long she'd have to wait for him to reach now? A blasted car! So he could *drive* to visit that good-for-nuthing ordinary girl from Cambellville, and take her for *drives*. He better not come to show off the car with *her* inside.

The sight of Bullet and Baby Doll on the shop verandah just made Emelda rush inside the shop, bramming the back

65

door violently. She served a customer at the counter from right under Ricardo's nose, slammed on the salt-biscuit tin cover and served three more while Ricardo dreamily dealt with one. The lines around her mouth became trenches. Baby Doll and Bullet hustled away as casually as they could and Mr DeAbro began to pay more attention to business.

Inside the dark shop, Emelda furiously shovelled flour into brown-paper bags, stirring up a cloud of white. Flinging the bags on to the scale and grabbing them off, scarcely allowing the weights to start rising. Not spilling any, sealing the small bags ... thump each one quickly, grab the top ends, fold and spin the whole bag once, then tweak the points down. One-pound bags, two-pounds, then bending half her body over into the big crumply flour sack, the five-pound ones. With every hair on her face and arms bristling white, she had done by seven o'clock and stormed back home through the night like a witch, without a word to Ricardo.

Hell knew was thunder in that house tonight. As soon as she hit the gate, the cusses rang out bout 'Ricardo and the fucking whoas'. Emelda was a lady that didn't cuss. She was a decent, very Catholic, respectable woman. That night she took a turn in everybody tail, even down to Theo who had already fed her chickens and collected the eggs. By nine o'clock she boiled down to a steaming tight bundle on the front porch, arms clenched around herself and legs pinned together. By ten she was a heap of sobbing rags on her bed, bawling shamelessly. By the time the older girls had rubbed her down with Limacol and tied a compress around her head, it was midnight and she was dozing fitfully.

The night's hysteria had long since driven Ricardo out to drink. Theo joined him. At two in the morning when Theo returned, the click of the gate latch raised the restless Emelda out of bed. She sat on the front porch, head still tied up, cool breeze rippling her yellow nylon nightie, until the sound from the shop across the road really sank into her head.

'Anne-Marie! Agnes! Your Fucking Father and the Fucking Whoas! Oh Lord, I gon kill him!'

She sprang upon Anne-Marie and Agnes like a bat, ripping them out of bed. Grabbing the mortar pestle in one hand and holding her head with the other, she was flying through the gate and over the road to the shop before they could stop her. Wailing and shrieking, lashing the side of the shop with the heavy pestle. The racket she raised reached every house around.

'I go fucking kill you! Is fucking pussy you want? Is fucking whoring, black pussy you want? Open de fucking door leh me break yuh neck, you dog you. Ah know you have dem inside dere. Open de fuckin door!'

Bram. Bram. Bram.

'Ah go mash it down dis night here, Ricardo. I fuckin ketch you!'

The girls were too frightened to go close to her and their pleas to not let people hear were long gone in vain. Just as Emelda started a fresh assault, Ricardo opened the door. Just a crack at first and then slowly, standing aside to let the frothing Emelda in. He looked flushed and rosy but calm. Glancing at his daughters huddled together in the dark yard, he turned and followed Emelda's banging and crashing trail back into the depths of the shop.

The racket strike-up full volume now, full range as the

pestle lashed from biscuit tins to wooden pickle-pork barrels, iron bunkposts to laminated countertop.

'Whey you hide de fucking bitch?'

Glass crashing.

'You ain talking?'

Aluminium sink clang.

'I know you have de fucking cunt in here!'

Countertop and tin-stock shelf.

'Is ghost you fucking now? Whey you have she?'

Emelda banged on but slowly the sounds got weaker and weaker. Till all you hear was 'Ricardoooo!'

Then Anne-Marie and Agnes moved in and came out with her. Not a sign. Not a sign of the whoa she knew was in there. Defeated on top of suffering her worst day and night. It was too much to bear.

Next morning fresh news in the market – Baby Doll name change to Sugar Baby. Was the sugar barrel – the one that had taken blows from the flying pestle. Ricardo had pushed her down in there and jammed the lid on. Weeks after that nobody ain buying sugar from DeAbro. Sugar Baby in demand and Emelda quiet. Too much to bear. Mums said it was a Nervous Breakdown, that's how-come the cussing.

Bullet was a different story altogether. She nineteen years old and six foot tall. Thick straight thighs and fat ankles. Hair natural and short, high broad shoulders and she always ready to laugh. Why she was called Bullet was from the times when she had a boyfriend. He was from Scheme and was a drug pusher, that's how she got a taste for the wild life. She was liming with him when some other pusherman was shooting him down. But he missed and she got the bullet in her pussy. True. She was in hospital to get it out and since then the name left on her – Bullet. And he the boyfriend, didn't even go and visit her in Georgetown General. By the time she came out'a hospital, he already had another woman and he tell Bullet how he didn't deal with damaged goods. The amount'a heckling she got on the street after that though, made her the hero. And she being spunky, took up the challenges and started showing man what bullet-hot pussy can do. Soon her reputation for giving a man the quickest, hottest fuck made her take it up full time.

She was the youngest and the freshest of the three and was soft still, even though she did the most business. Wasn't no hard shell on her. She walked the way any healthy nineteen-year-old girl walked down the street. Her small pointed bubbies bouncing under the thin white vest. Her shorts riding her firm backside. And everybody from my brother to Uncle Joe couldn't help watching her or calling out to her. She'd give the same twinkly smile and friendly reply to all. Was difficult not to like her. I liked her in the same way I admired my older sister's friend from town. She had that same big gangly but thickset way of walking and bouncing her bubbies. The bouncing said to everybody 'I like sex. So what?' But not in a hoity-toity way. This sister's friend from town was from a highbrow family. Bright too, went to Queens College. She liked sex so much, all the boys in that school and every friend she brought to our house had a familiar way of touching her. Bullet had it that way too. They so big bout their sexiness, was a joy to watch one a'them plunk herself down on a bench – big legs all over the place, big lips smiling, eyes squinged-up laughing.

*

Rumshop Cockroach was like her name said. No dignity there, no end to what she'd do for a couple dollars. She lived with a man, Clinton, and had a few young children. We never knew if Clinton was the father. They lived in a small wooden house behind the shed across the road. It had no trees around it, no outside bathroom or latrine. Just the closed-up weathered shell stood in the lot. In the morning Cockroach combed and dressed the children in the doorway and sent them off to school. And in the afternoon when they came home, Cockroach would sit in the doorway while they played around or looked for firewood.

Clinton was hardly ever home. He black-black and hard-bodied, a mechanic, a welder and somebody no one troubled. Daytime he'd walk silently in the hot sun covered with black grease. And night-time, skin shining, clean overalls, he'd put on dark green rectangular sunglasses with gold-coloured wire frames. Night or day, he always walked on the edge-edge of the road as if trying to avoid people. Never saw his eyes – in the day he looked down at his feet, at night with those sunglasses on, all you could see was the frames. One of his eyes wasn't working but not even my brother Yan and his friends dared call him One-Eye Clinton.

Rumshop Cockroach was hard-bodied too. Gaunt and sunken-eyed, her high hard belly stretched her dry skin taut. Her wasted arms and legs dangled wrinkled skin. Her toes'd clutch the front of her slippers and her spindly fingers were always ready to reach for the dregs of rum in the men's glasses. In her drunkenness she could'a easy lose the couple dollars she earned. But the men in St Kitts Rumshop looked out for her and wouldn't let her get beat up or ripped off by a stranger. She was always sliding around the dark galvanized walls of the rumshop but wasn't allowed in the 'hotel' rooms upstairs. That didn't matter to her though, behind the fence was good enough.

That day, the sound of flesh hitting flesh came from the closed-up house. The four a'we lined up inside the fence across the road, squatting, faces pressed between the staves of rough greenheart. A loud crash from inside sounded like a body falling. No screams, no crying, no shouting. And then a crack. He must'a broken off a leg of a chair or something. Sound of it hitting flesh and a high-pitched wail came seeping out the cracks of that house.

A small crowd had started gathering on the dirt street. Aunt Ruth, the obeah lady who lived behind DeAbro's shop, came out and brace-up on a coconut tree. Blows fell fast now and churgles and chokes dribbled out of the house. The door flew open, pitched out the children and slammed shut again. They stood one shaking bundle of skin and tears, blinking at the people on the street, then scrambled under the house into the mud. More thumping from inside. Sounded like wrestling. The children squiggled closer to-gether in the mud. A sharp, stinging, broad-hand slap on skin. And then another. We looked sideways as far as we could through the slats of the paling, to the adults. The men started moving off. Then deep grunts started, between the thumping. The choked sobs got more frequent and took on a new tone. We strained to see the adults' faces again. The women were looking guilty.

'He fucking she now,' Judy hissed.

'You lie!'

'No girl, listen.'

We cocked our ears, catching all the small sounds. It still sounded like wrestling but the grunts and sobs were getting

71

louder. Now and again the bang of a head or a knee on the floor rammed the children deeper into the mud. The sob-choking sounds started to rise at the ends. It was clear that it was fucking now and that it was going to finish soon, loud and embarrassing. The women started chasing their children and dragging them up the street. A few boys had caught on and were killing themselves with laugh, rolling around in the sand like real asses. Aunt Ruth signalled 'Come!' roughly to the pile of children under the house, then turned and disappeared with a disgusted steups and a flap of her skirts. The fucking sounds got louder. Fierce. The children untangled themselves and scuttled across to Aunt Ruth. A scream reached out. And then silence. Just the sound of our breathing and the strong smell of greenheart.

FOUR

Aunt Ruth the obeah lady made you shake with one look. I felt sorry for the children scuttling over to her. Lord knows what she would do to them now. That afternoon, Clinton and Cockroach's fucking done, we turned to what went on in Aunt Ruth's yard.

Aunt Ruth's small upstairs house was always curtained and closed. Underneath, there was a room, big fowl coops, baskets, a hammock and firewood. The shingled kitchen stood by itself a few feet away from the back steps. Inside was black from woodsmoke. The whole yard was smooth packed earth, immaculately clean. Cool and sinister. Any loose sand showed the brush marks of Aunt Ruth's pointer broom. Constantly sweeping. Sweeping the yard. Under the house. In the kitchen. With her other hand tucked up, resting on her bent back. The thing is, even though she was sweeping all the time, she didn't look as if she was paying any attention to what she was doing.

She was a strong, broad-shouldered, erect woman. Even

when she was sweeping, she bent from the hips and swivelled easily down to the ground, her skirts straight and bumsey in the air. Always had on a headtie. High cheekbones and a flared nose. Lips that had stretched and then shrunk hung and shook when she talked. You could know she was a obeah lady by the red eyes, blazing. A blood-sucking Old Higue too. Everything bout her had a dangerous ring to it. From her loud high-pitched laugh, mouth all gaps and gold stubs, to the way she puffed on her pipe, to the way she walked and swished those layers and layers of old skirts that never came off. One of Miss Nora children ended up underneath that self-same skirt. He was t'iefing Aunt Ruth genip and she saw him. Next day, swishing down the road like she didn't notice him, she just grabbed him and trapped him under there. The thing worked like a stink trap, he couldn't even bawl. Choking, cause nobody ever ketch her bathing and the fumes under there almost killed him. She gripped his hand through the skirt, swooped him right to her front gate and just let go as she went inside. You wouldnt'a even know she had a small child under there. He never told us bout it but her red eyes glinted now whenever she looked at one of us who saw it happen.

Later that year Popo and Ursie's child died from bad blood. Mrs DeAbro's granddaughter. Was Aunt Ruth that got the small coffin made and prepared and dressed the dead baby. Aunt Ruth had come over and talked quietly to Mrs DeAbro, then went about it like it was her business. I don't know how a obeah woman like Aunt Ruth came to be involved, Mrs DeAbro being a Catholic, but Theresa, the fair-skin, hoity-toity one of the family, raised hell and stopped the baby being taken to Aunt Ruth's yard. If Baby

Isabel had gone with her, she might'a just disappeared in that dark yard. And what came out might'a looked like Baby Isabel but we was sure that it wouldn'a been.

This was the first time we saw Aunt Ruth working her obeah. She picked up the child and held it in the crook of her arm, as if it were a living baby. The way she walked around Emelda's bedroom with Baby Isabel bundled up in her arm ordering things like a washrag and blanket, you could'a swear that soon you'd hear baby's cries. Baby Isabel was just starting to turn blue. Mrs DeAbro chased us all out the room soon enough. Had to content ourselves with whispering outside. She must'a had all the baby's clothes off. Pawing the bluish small body. Dribbling over it. Shaking those trembly lips. God alone knows what else she was doing to that baby, but she took a long time. We waited and waited, went to pick dungs and came back. Then she was done.

'Call Emelda.'

Emelda and Ursie came and we all entered the room. Wasn't no blood on Aunt Ruth's face or on the floor. Baby Isabel lay in her little coffin on the vanity, pristine and pure, her dress fresh and crisp, tiny sparkling black patent shoes and white frilly socks peeped out from under her hem. She still had her gold bangle on one wrist, and on the other, the cotton thread with the Hail'e Mary face that the priest had tied on. She must'a still had the little copper tube with the paper prayer inside it, pinned on her vest. Her skin looked soft and clean and she was smiling so slightly, like she might just open her eyes and twinkle them at you. She looked so happy. The surprise of seeing Baby Isabel like an angel in that box and the sun dancing round the room, bouncing off the mirrors of the vanity, melted Ursie.

Moaning softly, she slipped from Emelda's arm and crumpled to her knees.

'She peaceful,' Emelda said.

And as we stood there, all touching Ursie's shoulder, the vanity felt like an altar. Like it was holy. The long central mirror and two side ones made three reflections of Baby Isabel's cheruby image. The wood of the two drawers rose up on either side of the tiny coffin, like the altar was built for her. Her tiny gold crucifix glittered on her smocked chest. From somewhere behind, Aunt Ruth asked Emelda if she had two new cent pieces to put on Baby Isabel's eyes.

Aunt Ruth was the only woman in Tamarind Grove who dared disrespect Our Leader Comrade Linden Forbes Burnham. He was the Prime Minister who made himself President. Been in power for so many years now and things only getting worse. He, the government, owned everything and only PNC people got work. He give out so much jobs, all the government offices full'a half-asleep people. Cooperatives and Unions everywhere.

Outside the Co-op on Mainroad, Aunt Ruth had her place in the long queue but was strutting around on the edge of the road itself. The queue stretched from the Co-op door, past the butcher stall, almost to the front of the cinema. Women and children waiting to buy cooking oil and soap in eleven o'clock heat and dust. Burnham had banned imported goods and everything was a shortage. Mr DeAbro got so tired of saying 'We ain get none yet. No oil,' that he took the galvanized gallon measure and turned it upside-down on the counter, just had to point to it and turn up his hands. Sunlight soap, with its bright blue and yellow waxed wrapper, became a luxury item you could only get from hucksters or vendors. Only local-made Lux and Lifebuoy was sold in shops now but even they were in shortage, the ingredients having to be brought in. And although it said 'luxury soap' on the packet, with the pink complexion Lux Lady looking silky at you, it didn't feel so when that cheap-smelling soap was all the choice you had. We were a generation of Lux girls and Lifebuoy boys. Visitors or anybody going Away would now bring Camay and transparent Pears as gifts. We used them over Christmas or special holidays. As Mums got more fed up with what was going on in Guyana, I noticed she wouldn't keep her gifts to use at special times, she just used it anytime. Like it was soap, made to be bathed with not hoarded.

At the Co-op that morning we lined up with our oil bottles, sandwiched between bosoms and backsides. The Security Guard opened and closed the two doors, letting people in and out one at a time. All the people who worked inside there was from Tamarind Grove. But when they started bagging off precious flour and sealing bags of scarce milk powder, they behaved like they deaf and blind to people they grew up with. Sullen and sour-faced. Everybody working there had a 'position'. If they wasn't a Packer they was a Sorter. If they wasn't Supervisor they was Assistant. The place had three Managers. It even had a Janitor – somebody who does nuthing but sweep and mind people business all day. It had more workers in there than stocks on the shelf.

When you finally got inside, head hot from the sun, only the two cashiers and three customers in sight in the big cool building. On the shelves, all you saw was remnants from burst bags – split peas, channa, lentils, flour, salt, a sprinkling of sugar, a few loose matchsticks. Always some tins of

Baygon and Shelltox spray left, toothpaste and a few boxes of Fish Mosquito Coils. The Packers and Sorters lazily watched you walk towards them. When you reached them and stretched out your oil bottle, the sicky smell of cooking oil filled your nose holes as they poured in your measure. Only two pints per person was allowed today, and four cakes of soap. The Packers and Sorters watched you walk all the way to the cashier with the measly oil, watched you pick up the fat blue squares of soap before turning to look for the next poor person.

Miss Nora's eldest daughter was one of them Co-op cashiers. Aunt Ruth herself had pepper-douched her as a child. But now she had some Burnham power and was just like the rest'a them. When twelve o'clock reached, she was the one who told the Security Guard to stop letting people in. She would plop your soap into a paper bag, raise her blank face and push off her stool to go home for lunch. Outside, she'd pass the crowd, dragging her flip-flaps, leaving people waiting till she came walking slowly back at one o'clock.

From afar, a wailing siren signalled Burnham's approach and a grumble rippled forward from the back of the line. The black limousine stopped suddenly right in front of the Co-op, police bikes, with lights still flashing, circling it as Our Leader Comrade Burnham stepped out. His rosy face was smiling, big eyes dead, just like the photos on all the exercise books and billboards. He wore the Well-off African Politician look – grey-blue shirtjack over his paunch, black shoes glittering, gold band on his wrist. Escorts all around him, dressed the same, with dark shades on.

'Mrs Sampson, ah see you ain lose no size even with all dis hot sun. Yuh husband must'e strong! Heh. He don' need some help?'

Mrs Sampson, huge arm akimbo, shifted her weight and looked at the ground before looking back at Burnham. Heads craned to look at her then him.

'And Mrs Bee,' he went on, 'you did some good work de other day fuh Tamarind Grove. What *else* you does so good? What kind'a *work* you could do fuh me? Ah like a woman who does *hard* work.'

A couple'a women around Mrs Bee laughed and slapped her. Mrs Bee and Mrs Sampson was respected leaders in the village. I'd never seen them get like children so, shuffling around.

'Youall came out in full support at the People's Day Rally. I was impressed.'

'An is so you paying we? Makin we line up for every damn t'ing?' someone shouted from the front of the line.

'You shut yuh mouth, you almost reach inside already. What you complaining bout? Youall have to pay for education now? No. You have to pay for schoolbooks? No. Soon you wouldn't have to pay for school uniforms, *that's* what I doing for you – providing a future. What you lining up for now?'

By this time Aunt Ruth had sidled right up to Burnham.

'Cooking oil and soap,' she hissed at him.

He turned to look at her. She gave him a cut-eye from head to toe.

'Oil? Oil to cook with? You don't need to line up for oil. We have coconuts dropping off the trees in this country. And soap? You can wash you clothes with salt. Plenty salt around.'

Was the first anyone heard bout washing clothes with salt. Salt?

'Burn'am ...' Aunt Ruth rasped slowly, not moving, looking at him sideways, ' ... you full'a shit. You know what you can do? You can kiss my black stinking arse.'

FIVE

Today Rachel is Wife and I am Husband, Sammy is
Wife and Judy Husband. Sometimes we all just girls,
with towels over our heads for long hippie hair.
We'd put on my sisters' old bell-bottoms, our shirts unbut-
toned and tied in front, and practise pouting, slouching and
swinging our hips about. Or sit sprawled out, legs wide
open, pretending to smoke. A toss of the towel hair, chin in
the air and throat curved back, in that bored sexy way.

The battery felt cold on my bunge inside my panty. Judy
had a battery too. It gave me a very private feeling inside the
huge musty clothes. I'd found a blue shirtjack and a
threadbare pair of my father's beige corduroy pants. Tied
them at the sides with string. The wives had on old bras
stuffed with socks and pinned at the back, long dresses and
pink and blue towel hair. Judy and I donned our shoes –
they helped give an important feeling – and sauntered out
of the house to the busy city streets. Street was the upstairs
front room. We stood there chatting with our chins tucked

in and hands in pockets as men do when they talking bout important things. The fact that neither of our fathers went out to work on streets with pavements, or stood and chatted in this sophisticated way, didn't matter, as we braced against the windowsills, casually crossing a leg. In the world of movies, which is how real people live, this is what men do. Meanwhile inside, Rachel and Sammy was doing what wives do.

When I was a wife, I took pride in my housework. I didn't pretend – got down on my knees and buffed the whole floor of the houseroom. I put away the kitchen neatly, made the beds without a crease, always aware of my towel hair swinging and the socks inside the bra pressing on my flat nipples. Them women in the Gary Cooper films was boring. They didn't even do anything, and then all of a sudden, their house'd be spotless and dinner ready to serve. And when it came to getting down to business, they didn't even do that either.

As we stepped through the door from the hectic world of Wall Street, Sammy and Rachel hurriedly straightened their hair and dresses. We had timed our working day well, having been wives ourselves and knowing how long it took to clean the room. We pecked them gravely on the cheek, pretending to take off hats and hang them behind the door. In a wearied resigned way we mumbled about it being 'another day' and we all sat down to eat. Seated on the floor around the square piece of cloth that the girls had carefully laid with books, we picked up our pens and pencils and began to eat politely without further talk. The wives kept glancing at our expressions to see how good their cooking was. Wasn't bad, loaded with things we'd never eaten or even seen.

'This broccoli is lovely!'

'Whey de pork?' Judy snapped.

We all instinctively looked to the centre of the cloth for a second and then buss out laughing.

'This is a vegetarian meal,' Sammy said.

'Well how come we eating lamb?' Judy asked.

It was delicious anyway, but with so much manners the wives took for ever to finish eating. They was chewing with their front teeth, mouths closed, lips mincing like when somebody with no back teeth trying to chew one grain of rice at a time. The dishes were cleared away and washed on top of the chest of drawers, while Judy and I went about pinning up sheets over the windows. And then it was night.

Taking off everything but my panty and battery, I slipped under the sheet and watched the wives undressing. They took off everything, even bras and panties. As Rachel took off hers, the lumps of socks stuck to her flat chest. I thought she had the most beautiful body of all of us. She knew it too. Knew that it was the closest thing to the movie kinds. Me and Sammy, we were all arms and legs and Judy was athletic with a long body and hard powerful legs. But Rachel had a soft well-proportioned body, and small feet without a crease on them. I held the sheet up high as she climbed in. We all said good-night to each other and plopped and turned about in bed making settling-down noises. I puffed the pillow again and then slapped my head down on it. Rachel's back was towards me and the room was orange and warm. I stuck my head under the sheet and stared at the lovely swirl of light brown goldeny hair on the back of her neck just below the big neckbone. She knew it was time. Under the sheet she turned on to her back and wriggled an arm past my neck. Both our heads were together now, my chest and leg touching hers. I stroked her chest down the centre to her navel, following the fuzz, and felt my chest grow sticky and huge. We were looking at each other's faces now, up close. Eyes, nose, lips. She had more fuzz all around her mouth and a moustache of little beads of sweat. She was touching my eyebrow, breath coming out in small, sweet, warm puffs on the corner of my mouth. I shifted down slightly so my eyes were level with her mouth and peered into the dark pink crack. I could feel my moustache growing too. There was a sound of movement from the other bed and I quickly stuck my head out from under the sheet. Judy was on top of Sammy already! We hadn't even kissed yet. I pulled my head back in, rolling on to Rachel and wriggled up slightly until my bunge was in the right place and the battery was held between our two bones. We kissed now, hurrying, just pushing our lips together and keeping them there for a second. When I lifted my head and licked around my lips, she did too. Was strange, our sweat had mixed, wet and salty.

There was a thin layer of moisture all over us now. It sealed our stomachs and ended where our chestbones pressed together. As I pushed up on my arms and we craned to see what was happening down there, our skins peeled away from each other like parting layers of a wet plastic bag. The battery slipped to one side and I grabbed it through my damp panty and centred it again. Saving the battery, we kicked my panty down my legs to the bottom of the bed. Our skin was touching everywhere now. Hipbones touching, my thighs slipping on hers as I tried to put the battery back between our two bunges, and keep it there. Held her tightly. She wrapped her arms round my shoulders and we started rocking from side to side. This was when the battery'd always fly out. It slipped to the dip at the side of her bunge, I followed it with mine and we gripped tighter. Rocking harder. Rolling so much the sheet started wrapping around us on each side.

Her earlobe was covered in the stuff too, the fuzz. I put my nose in and smelt her ear. No smell, but it made her wriggle. I was a goat smelling its pee – pushed both my lips up under my nose and curled them open, wrinkling my nose and stretching my neck up. She was trying hard not to laugh, we rocking still. I plunged my curled-up muzzle into her ear and inhaled loud. A little yelp slipped out of her and ended with a shrinking squeal as I snuffed some more. Goosebumps! All the hair up her neck was standing. Pelting back the sheet we snuffed and skin-up our lips in the air, giggling and squeaking, feeling the little electric shivers raising hair. Judy and Sammy were still under their sheet, but laughing too.

'Sssh, youall making too much noise.'

We should finish quick now before anybody came and found us all naked. I'd forgotten bout the battery. Now I found it stuck under Rachel's bumsey. Holding the sheet up to my shoulders, I reached down and, seriously now, felt around her bunge to find her slit. She pulled her thighs together and it made the two lips feel fatty. Rachel tense, waiting, fresh moustaches springing out. We held the battery carefully, lengthwise between us. The flat end pressed on the tip of my pulsing slit, closing it, and the other end, the one with the bump, wobbled on the flesh just above hers. Levering up, I gently squeezed my bumsey in, making the battery push my flesh against bunge bone. The tiniest movements angled the bumped end of the battery so it didn't just press right down and hurt her. Held our breath, not looking at each other, concentrating, I could see the weave of the pillowcase four inches from my face. Hearts thumping, hips stiff, dripping with sweat. Moving the battery ever so slightly. Judy's head popped out, red and foolish with a huge grin. And as we turned our heads to look at her, it slipped. We collapsed laughing, gulping for air.

While we were dressing quickly, our faces shiny and wet in the orange light, me and Rachel showed them bout goat snuffing in the ear. We forgot about the hurrying and went on snuffing. Three short ones, curl your lip out, stretch your neck up, goosebumps and laughs. Three short snuffs, curl your lip out, stretch your neck up, goosebumps, try to keep a straight face.

Sammy and Rachel always fought over the remains of Barbie and Midge, the big sisters' hand-me-down dolls. They both wanted Big Bubbie Barbie – though she only had one leg. The loser would have Mash-up Midge, with her flat chest and only one arm. That left Ken, the man doll with no arms and a stupid expression on his face. And Cindy, the one we made with another doll's head and arms. Was a good white girl's name, we thought.

Big Bubbie Barbie always so sexy! Pushing up her bust all over the place and wobbling around tiptoe on her one foot. But her leg could swivel right up good. Mash-up Midge could do it too, and they'd skin-up their flat hard bunges anywhere. Sometimes you'd open the cupboard and find the two of them there, just skin-up, with they clothes up over they head. We'd drag them through the garden – Carry On up the Kyber, Big Bubbie Barbie squeaking, Ken silent and smiling. Sweating, climbing up the broad banana leaves, sticking in the mud. Sometimes for ski-slope adventure we'd visit the freezer. Keep the door open for as long as we could and rub their skin-up bottoms on the ice, Barbie bawling 'Thrilling!' Dash back upstairs and Judy or me'd take Ken and rub him hard on her.

'Oooh! Not so hard!'

Bang, bang, bang . . . the hard plastic knocking together, Barbie's hard bubbies beating his chest. Clack, clack, clack . . . hold them together in mid-air and spin them against each other.

'Oooh Ken, you're sooo wild!'

Midge'd take it good from him too – and not be talking so much stupidness. And even Cindy got it. But her legs couldn't swivel so good. Ken'd be with his stupid smile all the way through, like he just made to grind.

Dads brought home a new brown-skin Asian doll – Tamika. She was hot. She came with red panties and sarong, black long hair, stout and smiling with flashy dimples. She show Big Bubbie Barbie and them what dark-skin dolls can do. She had no top and a flat chest but anytime she ketch Ken, she give it him good!

'So vulgar!' Barbie squawked.

''Cause she more sexy dan you!'

'No! She's just like those, those . . . natives!'

And, movie-style, Rachel'd pelt down Barbie – flat on her face to howl and kick her one leg up and down.

SIX

After Iggy had made my bunge burn and quiver, I
walked around like I was carrying a bomb on me.
Should I ask Judy about it? She might know bout
things like that. But Iggy's her brother. And anyway she
might know bout things like what? It wasn't sex. Was just a
feeling, more like an embarrassment. Iggy didn't seem
embarrassed though. I kept well away from him but when
his eyes caught mine, they was wicked. Looked as if he
could just catch me anywhere and press himself on me
again. Made my bunge burn more.

Sex is the thing we saw in the book – *Man and Woman*.

'Look, look, look, you see! That is how the lolo does fit in
de pokey. You see?'

'Dat is how? Dat is how they does fit? Oh me Lawd!'

We had t'iefed the big grey book from the bookshelf
where it lived, innocently, between art books and ones
about nature – books that when you were allowed to look
through them, you had to do right there on the floor.

Couldn't take them off to your room. Them books was honorable, they felt expensive. When you lifted down the heavy ones, they had glossy dust jackets. Beautiful objects and places shone out at you when you turned the big clean ink-smelling pages. Things you could never even dream of. *Man and Woman* was the plainest, roughest, strangest book on that shelf. When I found it first time, it shocked me right back from the Sahara Desert where I was. I had it down on the floor in front of the shelf. The pictures! I scrambled it and shoved it back in its slot, purple with shame.

Now we examined every page carefully, safely inside our room with the door closed and a grey biology book standing in for *Man and Woman* in its place on the shelf downstairs. A big woman's ugly hairy slit lay spread open for the world to see. So ugly! My bunge couldn't look like that. It had folds and creases and a mountain at the top of the slit. Wasn't far from one'a them geography books with wrinkled-up land.

'You know you have all'a dat?' I asked Judy.

She was two years older than me and Rachel. Sammy was the youngest. But the way we stuck together it was me and Judy, Sammy and Rachel.

'Of course, girl, but it don't look like dat. You can feel it. You can't feel your Tip? At the top part? I looked at mine with Agnes's compact mirror, but it's not the same.'

'You saw dat? Dat t'ing there?' I asked, pointing to the Tip.

'Yes. I tell you, you could feel it. Feel it now.'

I pushed my hand down in my damp panty and touched where it was burning. Felt around. My finger touching the flaming Tip. It burnt more, felt like it might pee. I pressed it hard with all my fingers and clamped my legs together.

'But it can't look like dat!'

'I tell you, yours don't look like dat. Dat ugly.'

Mine was smooth, no hair or creases.

'I don't want mine to get like dat!'

Sammy and Rachel turned pages like mad.

'Youall stop roughing up the book.'

'Look!'

A baby's head was emerging from another slit. Photos lined up down the edges of the page, the slit opened bigger and bigger, till it was round and the baby's hair showing.

'Next page!'

Bigger still, till the baby's head was out.

'Eeee Gad! She go split!'

But she didn't split. On the next page was the baby with blood all over it and the umbilical cord cut. Before that drawings showed you it growing and growing, seeing through the mother sideways, frontways, and how it was joined on with the cord.

'It come like she shit it out.'

'Dat is how you come out, you know.'

'I know, but you think my mother pokey look like dat?'

'Of course,' Judy laughed.

I boxed her head.

'But wait! Wait! Look at dis lolo!'

'At least it not as ugly as dat woman slit.'

'You ever see you father own?'

'Yeah. De balls long down just so.'

The line drawing showed the tube down the inside of the lolo connected to the bladder.

'You mean he could just pee in she?' Rachel asked. 'Nasty, eh?'

97

'I find de whole business look nasty,' Sammy added, turning another page.

'The book nasty,' Judy put in. 'Our mother would never have a book like dat in our house. What youall doing with such a nasty book on youall bookshelf?'

'I don't know. Maybe Mums an dem don' know it's there.'

'T'eo does have dem magazines with all kinds of naked girls. And I saw one with dey slits skin-up just like in this book. But it didn't look so ugly. I didn't get a good look though,' Rachel said.

Judy continued 'I know, but he does have to hide dem. What if Emelda was to find dem?'

'Anyway, if a man t'ing look like dat or like Uncle Joe own, I not letting it come near my slit,' Rachel said.

'Neither me,' Sammy joined in.

I was still pressing my Tip in my panty. Iggy's lolo look like that? It felt so hard. A big hard thing like that going right inside a soft slit must be painful. It couldn't feel as nice as the strange burning feeling. Specially if it had all them ledges and veins and things. And his felt so big. Felt like it was the biggest, hardest muscle on him. He'd push that thing into Mrs Peters's creasey black slit. Must be very ugly and painful. And he would have to be on top'a her like in the drawing, but he'd be huffing and puffing. He'd like to hurt people with that big ugly thing, I could just tell.

But the ugliness of Iggy and Mrs Peters sexing in my head seemed connected to the size of my Tip. It felt bigger and hotter. That's what he wanted to do to me. Even when he was calling me all kind'a embarrassing names, shouting

'Bamboo in pants' loud on the street, that's what he wanted to do to me. He must be a Fucker, or what them fellars called a Mother Fucker. He doing Mrs Peters and her fat daughter. Had to be a Mother Fucker.

In the shower later, the cool water from the wall tap fell in a soft pulsing stream on to the inside of my thigh. Splashes and flying drops hitting my other leg, my belly and the yellow tiles. I pushed my hips up to the base of the tap, legs splayed up against the wall, hands gripping the tap-head. Had been the gentle drumming of that soft but solid stream of water on my foot that made me want that same feeling on my inflamed Tip. I shifted my hips slightly and the clear tube of water fell directly on to it. Arched my back a little to get the stream on that part that felt best. The flowing mustn't stop. Hammering on the top of the Tip while the bomb in me was growing, making my heart faster, muscles tighter. Bomb getting bigger. Oh shit! Somebody going to realize I running the tap so long. The flowing lolo can't stop. I should have turned on the shower too. The Tip going to blow off. Oh Me Lawd! My legs shot down from the wall and I clamped my thighs together. Heart bombing-up inside and trembles and jerkings running up and down my arms and body, twisting me up so. The water hit the hard tiles with a loud splatting and then a soft smacking sound on my stomach. I pulled myself up to turn on the shower. Couldn't do no more than let myself back down on to the floor, quaking. Lay with my back along the rust mark on the tiles, my head and shoulders flat under the cool shower spray. Had to breathe hard out of my nose to stay like that, with blood racing and my body cooling. Legs folded, relaxed, on either side of the tap.

Bombed out. Stayed like that another long time with my eyes closed, listening for anyone coming and wondering if I could bomb up again.

After that, the bombing went on whenever I could get enough time in the shower. The fear of somebody finding me like that with my legs up against the wall made it scarier. Better. That and the horrible image of Iggy and Mrs Peters's ugly parts – or her fat daughter's. The snorting, grunting pleasure Iggy breathed out climbed the yellow tiles with me. And the big tree outside the window just watching.

Dogs, donkeys, pigs, ducks. Every damn thing jumping each other. Cats fighting and pinning down pussy in front you nose. Didn't look much different to what big men talked bout.

'Ah hold she an' give she good! She only bawling for more.' Grab the crotch.

'You know how long she want dat? Well she get it good. Ooh boy! Dis engine can still drive good.' Squeeze the crotch.

'Is action again tonight you know. She like it too bad, ah tell yuh, boy. She say she ain get it since two months. Dat was ripe! Ripe an juicy. Boy, ah need some seamoss today!'

Couldn't be much different from what we saw. Something like donkey. They made so much noise and carried on so. In the middle of the day, when everybody quiet and drained out from the heat, Cyril's do'tish donkey longing-down his long-long lolo. Right down and bawling like a fool. Brazen so. Braying to wake up everybody and show them what hanging down catching fly. If he pulling the cart and one-eye Cyril beating him, it don't matter, down the road he gone for woman-donkey, nose blaring,

100

top lip skin-up. Not stopping till he reach. Woman-donkey running to meet him. Right there in the middle of the road, broad two o'clock sun. Feel stupid just watching them. Cyril running, bawling and cussing. Woman-donkey just taking it, while Cyril donkey weaving from side to side on his back legs. Six hooves stamping around. Until she had enough. Cyril getting closer, she start moving off, hobbling the do'tish donkey along behind her on his two hooves. Clumsy fool with his neck sticking forward. Then slipping off, standing there with his head and glistening black lolo hanging down.

Sometimes when he was peacefully eating grass across the road, moving slowly, back legs stretching before he shifted his weight, the long black muscle would start coming out. Slowly and quietly it stretched down till the tip of it was swinging in the grass. As he shifted, it swung with a rubbery movement. Wasn't much different from the glimpse I got of my father's, or Uncle Joe's lolo. Gave me a little bit of the bombing-up feeling. Made the clear-stream tap change to solid black muscle sometimes. That big thing and the bombing feeling, made a shame grow in me. Shame, if anyone was to find out I bombed up with it. Of somebody catching me with the long black muscle coming out of the tap and into me. It made the explosion bigger. Was something I couldn't explain to Judy.

Like the pigs. They made Iggy's humphing sound when they did it. They were huge and heavy and close to the ground. For all their short-crotch charging, was only a little wormy pink lolo that shot in and out. That couldn't do more than tickle the mother pig's huge pokey. Maybe it went in very far. Just like a long worm.

In the small street between the DeAbros' home and ours, we blocked off one end and Pike, the pig breeder, ran his prime father pig into the street. Theo, face glistening and tense, twitching a small whip in his hand, moved round his mother pig making grunting noises in his throat. She headed for the muddy drains. Theo blocked her. Pike's father start running after her. Huge black snorty beast, barely kept off the ground by his jiffling stumpy hooves. Ears flapping, snout jerking upwards with every step. Made the mother pig look small. Theo's favourite big white sow. Belly and nipples grazing the ground when she was pregnant. Theo was signalling to the father pig, crouching, looking him in the eye and making throat noises that sounded like 'up'. Leave it to him he'd just jump right on and do it himself.

'I tell you T'eo does fuck dat mother pig,' Sammy whispered to Rachel.

'We never ketch him!'

'Watch how he getting on. Lula, look.'

'He want to do it,' I said. 'He talks with dem, you know.'

Theo was still crouching and moving around the two pigs, them snouting each other, grunting and snuffling. His whip reached out and flicked their broad backs lightly, raising up the frenzy in them.

'He want it bad. Watch he face.'

'T'eo fuck dat mother pig already,' Judy said lazily, not moving her head. 'And de black one he have. And a couple'a dem small ones too.'

We looked at her and she looked at Theo through half-open eyes with her head raked back.

Mother pig stamping and shuffling around more now. Pike's father hefted himself up and across her back sideways. She shifted with him for a second before he slipped, thudded back down. A tap on his rump with the whip. Got a glimpse of a small piece of wet wormy lolo. He tried again, this time from the back, and hunched his rump in. Theo moved in front of the mother pig's face so she couldn't go forward as Pike's father scrambled clumsily to stay on, humping away. When he slipped off again a longer length of the pink wet worm was hanging. Theo urged him on again but the mother made a dash for the drain. Pike's father charged after her now, frenzied up, ears flapping. Theo moving out of the way. Knocked her around the head with his snout. She quarrelling, his big mouth open, stumpy back teeth showing. Humped her hard. She start screeching. Loud. It *must* be long. Screeching, mouth open and into the drain. His snout hit the muddy water, smack. Mud splashing all on the street. Theo at the edge of the drain red, arms waving. The two'a them pigs smudging around, throwing their heads at one another. Both big muddy shapes glistening and garumphing.

'Get de fuck out'a dere!' Theo thrashing his whip on bits of the pig he could reach.

'Iggy, bring de long stick.'

Theo poked at the big mud lumps. Jabbing them hard till the mother pig lurched out splattering great dollops of fresh mud. Pike's father set off after her and Theo went trotting behind the two splattering lumps, cussing and shouting. Halfway up the street the father blocked the mother, bit her snout and shoved her round. Hefted on and humped quick and hard. Her screaming, eye-whites showing. Breathing hard, Theo caught up with them, leant down and tickled the father's balls with his whip, making him hump more.

Judy looked at me sideways. The mud shapes screeched

and humped their way up the street to where Pike stood. When the father finally slipped off, Pike moved aside and let him continue his jerking-head trot, past him. Theo darted out in front of his mother with both arms raised.

'Oouts! Oouts!'

Blocking her and ooutsing her till she turned around snorting and plunked down the street to the mud hole again. Ran straight into it, puffing and sighing, blowing dents and bubbles in it.

Theo came slowly back towards the gate. He looked at Judy. She looked straight back at him. His beady black eyes took us all in. He smeared some mud across his forehead as he pushed his hair back, and stomped across the small wooden bridge and through the gate. Iggy garumphed. Slapped his thigh, laughed with us and winked, then slammed the gate behind him.

'Judy, you saw T'eo doing the pigs?' I had to ask her when we were alone.

'I heard. I can hear these t'ings. I not stupid, you know.'

'I know, but how you know is dat he was doing?'

'Because it sound just like when my father used to do my mudda. But is de damn pigs he doing downstairs dere. Late at night. He t'ink nobody don' know. But de way he look at me when I watch him, he know I know.'

'You ain frighten?'

'Frighten what? If he beat me, I go tell. He know dat. He too damn nasty.'

What Judy knew bout Theo was one more thing that made her hard. The more he glared at her, the more she hardened.

Judy didn't see what was so big bout the bombing-up feeling anyway. Said she could do it with her hand, easy. When I tried, it was too hot and rubby and sweaty. Couldn't hang and tremble like with the tap. As we compared the swelling of our nipples, not even breasts yet, and searched for signs of black hairs on our bunges, I noticed how Judy grew first. As the hair under her arms grew, the smell of her sweat changed. Her small breasts stopped growing and ours started. Her bumsey got bigger but she still could win races on the street, pumping them short big thighs and curving her long torso into a stiff jerking comma. Once she passed the finish line, she let go into a bouncing cruise, legs churning, separate from her body. Then she'd waddle home, rolling on her tiny feet.

When we bought our first bras, Judy already had her period. The whole lot of it. Every month. And she didn't even go on bout it. Wouldn't tell us much we didn't know already. She just went over to the shop for them big embarrassing blue packets of Lilly's for herself like nothing had happened. Something had changed though. The way the men watched her bumsey, they knew. She just longed-out her mouth more and gave them her sourest look. Her mouth became so long from looking serious that Rachel started calling her Long-Mouth Qwukwani. Her mouth set like the river fish's mouth. But was only Rachel that dared shout out 'Qwukwani' when Judy was winning races all the time. She'd have to start running herself though, when she let out 'Qwu...', and by the time '... kwani' came out she'd be under a rain of Judy's thumps and blows.

It must'a been the hairs and things growing on her that changed her slowly into a tough tight animal. Anne-Marie and Agnes made her do more work and she played with us less and less. That animal walk and snarliness about her made men's eyes hungry, her face harder. Made me know that she was getting closer to doing things she wasn't going to tell me bout.

Bright hot Saturday morning was cooking up the market colours and sounds to a boil. By mid-morning it'd be a plopping thick porridge, shrinking. By midday just a few burnt stalls and withered greens would be left – and the left-over market smell. We had a whole twenty dollars each. For two weeks, we had eyed the shining white pointed cups of various sizes and the cardboard price tags. This was something we had to do together.

'Make sure it's not too tight,' my mother said.

How I going to know that until I get home and try it on? Shifty and sticky, we'd already been up and down that end of the market till our legs was dull from stuck-on dust. We gradually got closer and closer to the blue tarpaulin spread with bras and panties. Luckily it was the last stall and on safe ground, right outside Teacher Dolly's front gate. The Indian stallholder and her son were sheltering from the sun in the back of their van, keeping an eye on their goods.

'I don't know why she have to have de boy selling panties.'

Huge ones spread out in front of us. Gigantic nylon balloons laid flat. All kind'a colours but mostly pale blue and yellow. High-waist jukebox ones. Bikini stereo ones. Frilly rosette-bumsey baby ones. All nylon.

'You don't want nylon ones in this heat,' my mother had insisted when we asked if we could have stereos instead of cotton jukebox panties. 'Cotton is much better.'

But Judy and Rachel had nylon ones. They stuck on to their skin and looked sexy, they looked sexy hanging on the line too. Not like our stretching soggy sacks. But the brassières – how to choose the right one? The Indian boy had laid them out since early. All the cones in glistening snowy white rows. From mountains at the back to eggshells at the front.

'Look, dey have ones dat can even fit Sammy. She have nuthing.'

'Mums didn't give her no money for no bra.'

Judy picked up one from the second row.

'What you doing with dat?' Rachel hissed. 'You don't even have so much.'

Judy's mouth got a little longer and she put it back. Me and Rachel picked up two from the front row. The cups was stiff and had circles of stitching round and round on them.

'How we supposed to know which one will fit?'

The woman was walking towards us, wiping her hands on the piece of cloth tied around her square hips.

Judy picked up another one. 'You have to try it on.'

'Where, here? You mad?'

'Over your clothes.'

'And look like a fool in front of all dese people?'

'Youall know what you want?' the woman asked, wiping her mouth on her sleeve.

107

'We want to know which ones will fit,' Judy said.

'Dat small-cup one you have in you hand.' She flicked her hand at the bra. 'Is de chest you have to check.'

'Where? Here?'

'Uh huh. Over your shirt. Jus check de chest.'

We turned away from her with the shining bras in our hands, huddled together as if we could form a room.

'Why youall don't go inside Teacher Dolly yard?' Sammy asked. 'Ask de lady.'

'You ask.'

We turned around, churning Sammy out in front. The woman looked at Sammy's chest.

'Excuse me, can we try them on just behind that gate there?'

The woman turned and looked at the gate – chainlink wire, completely see-through. Shrugged her shoulders in a sort of yes and started rolling her way back to the van as we hustled to the gate, gripping the bras.

Three of us braced on the gate forming a wall. One by one, we tried on the glaring things over our shirts. By the time we had paid the woman and waited for her to wrap each one in newspaper, they were already our private treasures to hurry home and gloat over.

First we had to get rid of all the Saturday-morning dust and the dirt from all the hands that had touched them. Watch them drying in the sun on the line, sparkling, swinging in the breeze, so new. And then at last to walk down the road with a brassière on. Strapped-up and stiff like a harness, but not much to put in it. Racehorses, prancy like. No feeling of shirt on your nipples, a hot space there instead. Looking down and seeing sharp points sticking the shirt out. And before that, the new figure in the mirror. Looked best with a loose white T-shirt with sleeves rolled up. Casual. We galloped around on the road all that evening, checking each other's chests when we faced the wind.

SEVEN

Mr DeAbro used to beat the boys and Mrs DeAbro would beat the girls. He used a piece of garden hose or a belt and she a wild cane. Sometimes the boys'd get beat together – Iggy, Manny and Bernard. The bigger brothers would help catch them and bring them forward.

'Was a shame that parents did these things to their children,' Mums'd say.

Never heard my father talk about it but he was the one who was Follower of Mahatma Gandhi – non-violence, no cruelty to animals, soya and long hair flowing. We got put in our room for punishment and the whole village thought this was ridiculous, a joke. I'd be waving and signalling to my friends from my window upstairs. People wondered why two educated people like Mums and Dads was so stupid when it came to straightening a child. I never felt a hard slap in my life but quaked at the pointed fires that sprang up in my father's eyes when he got mad.

111

Getting Mums mad was worse. She'd make you feel like you let her down, like you're not even honest to yourself and only worth a little of her pity. She didn't get vexed so easy though. She filled our lives with an everyday kind of strength, making us just glad she was there. Dads, he was the difficult one, so we avoided him and tried to find pleasures in the chores he'd set. Mums helped us look at the funny side of his do-good schemes. Was much more to see and learn though, through our windows, across the street. In other people's yards.

We were playing hopscotch on our bridge when Mr DeAbro zoomed past pulling off his belt. Rachel froze, balanced on one foot, bent to pick up her stone. Judy started running after her father, as if sucked in by the air he moved. Rachel had turned white. We all started slowly down the small side street to the DeAbros' gate, half not wanting to get there. As we crept through the gate and on to the front steps, the belt in Ricardo's fist struck and coiled around one of the wooden house posts. It whipped itself off with a rasping sound then snaked on to the fence, then a barrel. Smacked on to the concrete ground, pulling the cursing raging Ricardo around after it like a mad bull. We huddled as close to the top of the steps as we could, with Rachel in the middle. Eyes big. Sammy gripped on to me and Judy's face set, not going to cry. Iggy and Bernard stood still like two of the house posts, waiting. Was just about getting dark.

'And what de fuck de pigs ain get feed for, eh?' Ricardo spat out, frothing and jerking from paling to post. 'No water since morning!'

He drop a lash on the bottom step. We jumped. Rachel started snivelling. Iggy and Bernard looked at Ricardo ricocheting around the place. The two a'them stared at him, eyes alone moving, bodies braced. Like he was the one that had done something wrong. He wasn't man enough to beat them? What he had to get on like this for? Like a fool. Making himself an ass.

'Bernard! Get yuh tail here.'

The first blow fell on his back as he ran into it. His small wiry body span round, arms folded over his head, as he took another one cross the back of his legs. Rachel tucked her head in now and Judy's eyes glazed. I looked up over to Mrs DeAbro who sat steeled on the verandah and at Theo standing silent by the back steps.

'When . . . you . . . going . . . to . . . *fucking . . . learn?*'

The snaking strap fell after each word. It was getting dark fast now. Gloomy light under the house. Bernard's face dribbling. Small cries came out as he, Ricardo and the belt hurtled round the posts. Filled the whole of the bottom-house with the pig punishment.

'Iggy!'

He didn't have to say more. Iggy was there, ready. Ricardo, dripping and panting, wound the belt afresh round his fist and they looked each other in the eye. Iggy was as tall as he was and almost as big.

'Turn round!'

Iggy turned his broad back slowly towards him. Ricardo drew himself up, wiped his forehead with his sleeve, and brought the strap down hard across Iggy's back. Iggy flinched, flexed his shoulders and turned his head to look silently at his father.

'You want it . . . eh? I know . . . you will . . . do it . . . *again!*' Ricardo, struggling, hit harder.

Another stroke. Another. The tip of the belt licked across

113

Iggy's neck and his face snapped sharply to the other side. Sammy's grip was hurting my shoulder.

'Bring de fucking hose, T'eo,' slurred Ricardo, swaying slightly.

Mrs DeAbro jerked off the seat and ran inside screeching 'Oh God Ricardo!'

Rachel and Sammy stumbled into the house behind her, choking. It left me and Judy cold on the steps by ourselves, an empty step between us.

Theo returned with the length of hose. Ricardo grabbed at it, his strength returning. Iggy turned to watch him then he swung around, looked straight at me. Straight through the half-dark at me, his bottom lip shining. Looked down, hunched. Stiffened his shoulders again. Made them broader for the full force of Ricardo's blow. It came singing down with a hollow sound, ringing as it struck.

'You don't hear!'

Iggy let out his breath. Shifted then tensed again.

'You don't feel!'

The sound rang from the near darkness straight into Judy's hard profile. Ricardo made the blows take for ever, grunting and shuffling between them. Iggy's breath stopped then snorted out after each lash.

'Come here!'

Ricardo grabbed Iggy and shoved him around to face the steps. I caught his eye as he gripped a plank two steps below me. Ricardo was bringing the hose down on the back of his thighs and arse now, pausing for longer spaces in between. Every lash he took, Iggy rocked forward on to his toes. His waist dipped in and shoulders pushed up, head hanging from his great neck, curls jumping as the hose rang out. Suddenly Ricardo pelted the hose to the ground and retreated, heaving into the darkness. Left Iggy leant over, quivering and gripping the step. His whole body shuddered in waves, sweat glinting on his hairy forearms and dripping off his chin. My legs were locked together, squeezing. When he turned his head to look up at me, his eyes saw everything. With his face swollen like that and his black shape still shuddering in spasms, he looked right into my thumping heart and squeezed-up thighs. Felt myself get hot with shame. But, before they swung back down, his eyes seemed to soak it in for later. Like if he could, he might hold me right there and press his hard thing into me and keep it there. And keep on holding me tight.

EIGHT

I watched Iggy's spriggy-hair hefty man-self. He had an ease with it. Some other boys did too. Not like the hard black-black Rastas silhouetted in the streetlight. They were slinky cats moving into the night, their bodies liquid, rolling on to one foot and then the other, cool. They held their man-self tighter inside them, coiled, ready to spring. I gauged how much of that cool I could really get right, practised the walk. But all that really came off was the stance – legs apart, bounce-me-nuh look. All the nights I studied their movements from the upstairs window – the way they pulled on the bright cigarette stub and then swung down the hand, grab the crotch, shift to the other leg. That stance was all I could honestly imitate. But I could do it anytime I wanted to, even in a dress, and feel my man-self standing like that. Didn't matter that I didn't have a lolo muscle. Didn't have things that girls have either – small feet and smooth hands. My bunge bone looked like it was about to grow a muscle anyway. I could climb trees as high as any boy. Had corns across my palms from swinging on branches. Judy had a man-self too. Could climb good. She could hang on for longer with her strong arms and pull herself back up. When we played Dungs War and one of her dungs hit you, it stung hard, like was one of the boys pelt it. Rachel and Sammy, with their eye-blinking selves, always howled when she pelted them.

Some of them big men's man-self was sloppy. It just hung around in the flab round they waist. Jiggled in their shaking thighs and big bellies. Came out in a belch or a too-loud laugh or a slap on a woman's arse rolling by. Others held it stiff in their muscles, like Night Helicopter the watchman at Enmore Estate. When he walked down the road to work he strapped in some of his man-self with a big broad leather belt over his khaki shirt. The thing was pulled in so tight, looked like he wasn't going to breathe till he got there, two miles down the road. He'd roll from leg to leg, an aluminium saucepan of food in one hand and his baton in the other. And if you couldn't see his man-self then, puffed up like that, you couldn't see it in nobody. Yan and his friends dared each other to shout out his falsename at him – 'Night Helicopter!' – to see him let out his breath, let go of his man-self and run mad. Beef was like that too, charging his way through to the Co-op to unload sacks of flour. Hell to trouble. He was short, and square solid muscle. Always barged his way down the street, a belt round his waist too, even if he didn't have a shirt on. Belt on his bare belly and pants tied up below. Might knock you down if you didn't make way for him.

Look-Back had his man-self so covered up it was confusing. He'd walk and look back. Small mincing steps and look again. Bird movements, his long neck swivelling, his hands jerking everywhere when he talked, eyes darting. Pants belted right up on his chest. The Rastas had a different name for him. They called him 'Anti-man' and he'd scuttle past them fast and into his street.

I looked at my brother's man-self. It was like he was just beginning to know he had it. Maybe I could see it better than he could. It was wobbling around in his voice sometimes and making his apple begin to bump out. His hands gripped too hard and surprised him, growing feet kept stumping out toenails. His belly called for more and more food and his man-self came horsing out of his big teeth as he wolfed a whole loaf of bread down, laughing at how much he could eat. Dads must'a noticed it too. Gave him the keys to bring the van into the yard. Let him go to the cinema anytime he wanted, by himself. We had to go with one'a *them*. I was jealous that Yan didn't have to wear a shirt – my chest was flat as his – so I started walking around without one. Just wore a pair of Dads's old pants held up with string for braces. I began to hate Yan's man-self but wanted to stick around him all the time to do the man-things with him.

This was serious business. Our van had to have an engine job and then a body job. Yan and the boys were taking it on. Mikey, Neighbour Mildred's son, was in charge. He was a mechanic. I sat among the black hands and gasoline smell passing spanners. Had the whole range of them laid out in front of me. Half the time I'd be peeping into the dark under the van to where Mikey lay with a torch, trying to see if I could guess which spanner would be needed next. Carburettor was out, loosed apart. Yan explained how it worked. Took his time to teach me how it all went together while Son and Manny greased down parts of the engine.

121

Later, when I explained this important carburettor set-up to Dads, he smiled like he saw a little of my man-self. Squatting, grinning and greasing with the boys was the best times of simple man pleasures. When they put the engine back in and the sanding began, was even better. They gave me a small dent to sand and fill. I knew I could do it just as good as anyone, feeling it all the time with my fingertips. Was heaven busying up myself with them. The filler smell and hosing and water-sanding. Rubbing my hand on the smooth-smooth surface, sanding again. Laughing when they laughed. Not talking too much, just glad to listen to their shit talk.

I enjoyed my man-self with the boys. Bits of their man-selves soaked into me and I learnt then how to understand the man-self language. Like with Ramesh, flitting from the Great Van Job to his yardwork. His man-self was so soft and gentle and warm, it hurt me to see Dads shouting at him. Or to see him looking at Yan, shame showing on his face for not knowing so much. I knew I could try out how my she-self worked with him and he'd never embarrass me. I could trust him. My eye-contact could bring a faint smile to his mouth.

Or Son who was still a sparkly red boy. The only son of Mr Baker, the quiet hard-working house painter, and his warish wife from Buxton. Son had broad flat features and glowing skin, and lips that spread into a smile just as easy at me as at Yan or Manny. His man-self was something in his skin and shone out in a friendly comfortable way.

Iggy's brother Manny ignored me. He stored his man-self in his head. It grew as he got older, right there in his head. Made his head big and his hair long. Fancied himself and thought he was well spoken. It made him study and read till he was almost blind.

Mikey was tall, dark and lanky. Black slinky cat but white teeth smiling. He never knew how much I watched his man-self, his tall loose laughy way, made me want more of it. Be near him all the time. Walk and lope around with him. I watched the way he towered over his mother, looked after her since his father's death, protected her from the jumbies in the cemetery on the other side of their fence. And laughed with her about it. Wished I could come out of 'Yan's little sister' skin and be out on the street late when he came out bathed and dressed for the night. I'd whistle at him from the upstairs window and he'd whistle back before looking up. It always made him laugh and wave. Damn Buxton Spice laughed and waved too – mocking me. Had seen me practise stancing in front the mirror in the bedroom. Held in its breath, bent back laughing quietly then craning forward to see my eyes as I followed Mikey's silhouette up the road.

As I was learning the man-self language, I understood Judy's hardness better. But in Sammy I could see no man-self at all. Out'a the four a'we, she was the delicate one: legs skinnier than mine, turned-up mouth and eyes that could blink good. She had a way that could make you give her anything she wanted. She knew I recognized it and, later, when she got to growing her she-self, she'd flash her long straight she-fingers in my face – nails already growing – just to irritate me. She didn't want to miss out on anything even when me and Judy played as rough as we could to try to stop her joining in. Saskia was only two years younger than her but the two a'them couldn't be left in the same room for long. In no time Saskia'd beat her up or t'ief her books or something. Saskia must'a seen that 'get what I want' shape of her mouth or look in her eye. Sometimes I felt sorry for

Sammy. Guilty bout how we'd use her to get to go to the cinema and then treat her like she really too small to come. Never felt sorry for too long though. At the dinner table, she'd be giving everybody news. Miss Guyana Broadcasting Corporation: who buried today, who went to the funeral, where the grave is in the cemetery, what the dead face look like. Things we all saw together, she'd be letting out without knowing it. Got us in trouble too. If that was what she-self was all about, I go keep my man-self till I old.

NINE

Sitting in the back of the yellow van under the house, feeling things changing right here in ourselves. New sex parts growing, hot things running through your body. A new stubborn man-self growing in me. Judy with her born-in man-strength longing-out her mouth, making her more silent. Sammy blinking her eyes more, not knowing why, and Rachel, coming out from under her hair, beginning to behave like she should be favoured by her father, brothers, mother, fellars, friends – cause she looked closest to what people from Away look like.

It was mid-afternoon and still hot. Boila rumshop was playing one of his early Marley records. We knew all the words of Boila's ten records. Sometimes the rumshop had 'Saturdaynite Fêtes', but not this coming weekend. Uncle Joe shuffled past on the far side of the road, hanging his head, holding up his pants with one hand. His big feet stirred the dust between the asphalt and the grass edge.

'Uncle Joe,' Judy yelled, just cause she didn't have nuthing else to do.

He waved timidly and shuffled a little faster. A stray dog passed, following his nose off the road into the drain.

'Rice eater,' Judy muttered.

Sammy's heels were banging against the flap of the van tray. She was growing fast – bamboo legs shooting quick. She and Rachel dressed the same, had on shorts today. Mrs DeAbro kept telling Rachel to stay out of the sun. Maybe she'd end up pasty white like her older sister Theresa, and her two children.

To Mrs DeAbro's disappointment, Theresa had married a mechanic, a Rodriguez too, from the other Portuguese family in Tamarind Grove. He repaired old cars right under their house. Theresa and John had known each other since childhood, maybe even related already.

'At least is a Putagee,' Emelda consoled herself.

The Rodriguez family had more money than the DeAbros. Lived on Mainroad in a bigger house, had more overseas children and grandchildren. But Mr Rodriguez was far-gone with the rum. 'Alcoholic,' Mums said. He liked to sing 'I can see clearly now the rain ish gone . . .' staggering down the road with a bottle. ' . . . I can shee all obstacles in my waay . . .' Mr Rodriguez was Ricardo DeAbro's closest friend. Mrs Rodriguez stayed indoors mostly, busy with 'Elizabeff', her retarded tied-tongue daughter. Unlike Emelda, she made no bones about wanting to live in Canada. She had no feeling for Guyana or Tamarind Grove. She was almost Away already. Anyway, Theresa and John moved into the perfect little house next door to his parents. Now Theresa lived like them, raising her two 'white' (not Putagee) children without ever letting the sun touch their skin. Nursing them through their endless colds. Stuffing them till their stomachs were distended, trying to fatten them up.

Rachel looked like she was heading in Theresa's direction. When she wasn't with us, she started walking with her head straight, not smiling. She even began to spend more time with Theresa, helping to look after her ugly children. I figured her sisters wanted her to be like them and enter their world of white-trunk legs, permed hair, pimples and Portuguese boyfriends. She had more chances of that than Judy. Right now, she had her hair in two long plaits like me but it was light brown, almost *blond*. When her older sisters loosed it out, they were so proud of it. Of how straight and silky it was. I admired it too. Specially when she ran or jumped around. It glittered in the late-afternoon sun and would help us all feel more beautiful, playing in our dress-up dresses ready for some family party or outing. I would loose-down my hair too, black curls bouncing when we jumped. And together, clean hair springing and flying, smelling of shampoo and My Fair Lady powder, we were in fairyland – in one a'them books or films where was only soft light and nice smells and pretty barefoot children, playing among trees. We'd be glowing and rosy and warm.

Anne-Marie was half proud but half jealous of the attention Rachel's hair got when it was loose. She'd pull and tug at it and plait it so tight, Rachel'd be looking like a Chinee. Judy had long-time cut off her own hair – to escape the torture of combings and the beatings to make her sit still. She preferred to take the one big cut-tail beating she got when she chopped it off – and then to be left alone and called ugly. Judy was hard-skinned and secretive and that made the older sisters pick on her even more. And if they saw the smallest cut-eye flirt with black-black Mikey, or her walking down the street in front of him knowing that he was watching her shorts and then smiling at him, they found a way to give her more work. Made her do some nasty job, like cleaning the ringworm drains in front the yard. I know Judy like black man. I even heard Emelda shouting at her about it. But she won't tell me nuthing now.

I looked at her wiggling a loose paling in the fence. She was fed up, more bored than the rest of us, with the hot afternoon. She spotted a lizard on the crosspiece that ran the length of the fence and looked around for a long grass stalk to catch it with. Judy like black man, eh? But Emelda would never let her marry one. She had her own kind of man-self – maybe she just wanted to *be* like Mikey. He treated her like a boy most of the time. Or maybe she was after him? My Mikey? What she going to do – shame Emelda? Judy liked my brother Yan too. I knew it. All the tomboy antics couldn't hide it. Always hanging around the boys by herself now.

Sammy was still kicking the back of the van with her heels. Judy made a lasso with the grass stalk and crept towards the lizard. Got close enough to hold the loop of grass two inches in front of the lizard's face and froze. He wasn't moving either. Rachel touched Sammy's leg and her kicking stopped. A quick jerk of Judy's left hand sent him speeding into the trap and all in the same movement she swung it into the air, lizard jiggling madly, grass loop cinched around its waist. We were off the van before she could swing around, keeping the van between us and her in case she threw it at us.

'Wha wrang wid youall?' was all she could half laugh out. 'Come, come, come. I wouldn't do nuthing. Serious.'

She looked too bored to be lying, but you could never tell with Judy. Specially recently. We'd all learnt the hard way. We crept back to our seats cautiously, keeping our eyes on her. She was plopping the lizard along on the ground, bouncing him like a puppet on the concrete.

'Leh we go cinema tonight nuh?'

'During the week?'

'Yeah, man. Wha's showing?'

'Two Chinee,' I filled in.

Going to the cinema would make the weekend come quicker.

'Well, let's go,' Judy said, as if we could just ups and go anywhere we wanted.

She liked to talk like that, like she was a big man. She plopped the lizard along some more.

'I'll ask,' Sammy volunteered. 'Yan and Manny was going to go sometime dis week anyway.'

'Mammy would never let us,' Rachel whined.

Judy gave her a sickening look. 'Maybe if *you* asked her. Or get Manny to ask her.'

'And where we finding de money?'

'Ask your father,' Judy replied. The whole thing had nothing to do with her.

She had spotted another lizard on the fence now and swung hers up on to the crosspiece to face it. Her lizard was panting, greeny-brown stomach puffing in and out. We slid off the van and along the ground to get closer to the arena. Judy half crouched with her arm out. New Lizard was older, browner and bigger than Judy Lizard. Started swelling up his throat, pushing his head higher and higher in little jerks.

Judy Lizard panting less, Judy still holding on to his grass leash. New Lizard flaring out the last bit of his throat flap, his long toes spread out, gripping the grey wood. His tail stiffened, curving the tip into the air. Judy Lizard turned his stunned head slightly to look at us for help.

'Leggo de grass,' I whispered.

Judy just turned her head slowly to look at us squatted there – frogs in the theatre. In that instant New Lizard flashed forward and grabbed the snout of Judy Lizard in its mouth. So quick, all you saw was a flash of pale open jaw and then, with a splat, there were two tails thrashing around on the ground. Judy joined us hopping around on our haunches. Tricked out of her catch, she wanted her lizard to lose.

Last minute that afternoon we got the go-ahead for the cinema from Dads and Mrs DeAbro. Fighting-up to get into the new bras and clean jeans, hearts scrambling with excitement about going out officially at night. We going along with all the fellars with their loping, curling walks, some dressed-up and clean-smelling. Clutching tamarind balls, pennacools and bubblegum, we reached inside the cinema and filed off to our side of the half-empty House, away from Yan and Manny. Heads swivelling to see who had come with who and what they had on. National anthem started, we stood up with heads straight, eyes searching for victims in front and below us in Pit. As the lights went out people were still feeling around for their seats. Pit was mostly full. Rows of shoulders shuffled and settled on the long benches.

'You see who dere?'
'Who?'

'Da pickey-hair Rasta boy, de young one.'

He was one of the cleanest Rastas, just starting his locks and still living with his mother, not with them others down Backdam. Had sparkly eyes and dimples and walked smiling like he was carrying his own man-secret.

'He an' he friends.'

'He friends not so nice, you know. Dem is de ones dat t'ief Aunty Babe bhagee and ochroe.'

'Yeah, den dey tell her "Jah will provide."'

'Un huh.'

We shouting over the car-screeching racket of the 'Coming Attractions'. Cocking up feet and slouching down in the hard chairs, we sucked at melting pennacools and dissolved pinches of peppery tamarind balls in our mouths, saving the tamarind seeds in our sticky palms. Next 'Coming Attraction' was a cowboy movie, the star riding up to the screen with twanging music and then the beating-up and shooting – a must for everybody. From Pit, thumps on the back and shouts of approval only died down when Chinee names started jerking on to the screen and scratchy music blurted out at a deafening pitch. The smooth-faced men and pouting gliding women seemed to have no connection to the harsh nasal English of the soundtrack. Startled faces and bright red lips moved ten times before you heard 'Oh!' Soon they started edging towards the surprise ambush in the bamboo patch. Shoulders hunched and bodies shifted in Pit. Seatbacks breathed as people in House leant forward. And then the screeching tchac and chop attack began. Whistling somersaults and kicks flew over our heads and bounced around in the dark. Echoing. More blows caught the googly-eyed lover's head, knocking it from side to side. The music behind the screeches and

133

tchacs got louder, changed rhythm, and Master of Shaolin appeared. The jeering and hooting in the cinema became one shout of recognition and a Pitload of excitement helped him deliver his first kick with a roar.

'Heh! Heah!' we fuelled the Master's first strokes. 'Get up! Sit down! Whutucks!'

The bandit thrashing around and scrambling to get away now.

'Ketch he!' rang out.

'Hee!' A kick to the ground.

Bandit scrambled up again. Every silhouette in Pit helped block him. Some standing, some leaning.

'Heah . . . Heh!'

Fists smacking palms, hands slapping knees, feet stamping – he got finished off spitting blood in spasms into the dust. Powder-cool Master, with one flick, coiled his pigtail round his neck and stepped back into the bamboo.

Two more encounters with Master of Shaolin and the air became warm and moist. Sharp strong sweat and cigarette smoke steamed up from Pit. Glowing red butts jerked around. Wet foreheads and teeth gleamed. Adjusting our eyes, we craned forward searching for Pickey Ras.

'Look, he dere.'

He was directly below us. Judy pulled out her rubber band, looped it round her fingers and shot a tamarind seed straight at him. We rocked back, faces blank, staring big-eyed at the fluorescent screen, feeling it shining on our cheeks as he turned and looked up at House. On screen Pouty Mouth was looking at Master sideways, head bent down into her kimono.

'Pssst! Pssst!' One of the boys by the door was first to see her shoulder appearing from her kimono.

She turned and her back slid out of it, then she disappeared behind the red curtains around Master's bed.

'Steuups.' Somebody let out a long suck-teeth.

'Whoo, boy! Pssst!' at the moving curtain shadows.

We shot out bout five stinging, well-aimed tamarind seeds but the cussing didn't start till Master and Pouty Mouth had finished their feel-up. While the fellars pushed and shoved, accusing each other, we scowled at the screen, not seeing a thing. Nudging each other and pointing at the screen as if noticing some important detail. Smirking and pinching each other's legs, clacking knees together to keep in our joke. The final big fight took the fellars' attention and after a blaring crescendo of hoots, clapping and screeching the intermission lights came on. Sat there stunned like Judy's lizard, blinking in the warm, musty, suddenly huge cinema. Down the steps we followed the herd, to the roadside where vendors sold ice-drinks and channa. People drinking and arguing over the plot of Master. Around the side exit of Pit, men holding cigarettes in their mouths peed against the wall. Caught the eye of Pickey Ras – him cocking his head back, smiling, knowing it was us.

Ansa's wife and two daughters were peering down from the top-floor balcony watching the crowd. Ansa was the owner of this cinema, an Indian from somewhere near town and different – not a country coolie with coconut-oiled hair. Was the only one in that family trying to make things work. Dashing about, running up and down the steps of the three-storey wooden building, he tried to get the projector man to fix the projector. Tried to operate it himself when the man left the job. Tried to cut and join the film. Tried to get his town-boy son to stay in the projector room. Always wiping his forehead and pushing his flicky hair back. The cinema made him turn grey, right there and then. Balcony had never opened. Nobody had money to go so only the Ansas looked down from up there.

He could never get it together. Never get it right. And the minute the film jumped, where it was cut, steups and cusses shot up to Balcony. When the film stuck in the projector and burnt slowly on screen, the whole cinema bellowed 'ANSA! Fucking coolie!' Whistles, 'oayh's, palms slamming on benches and feet stamping. Until the lights came on or the film started again. Once, when someone pelt a stinking conga egg into the centre of Pit and everybody stampeded out, was Ansa that came with buckets of soapy water. As he scrubbed, embarrassment came from Balcony, jeering and disgust from Pit's doorways, pity from House.

Ansa spent so much money renovating the cinema, he had to make it work.

'You t'ink dese niggars appreciate dat?' Neighbour Mildred said to Mums.

She sold custard-blocks outside Ansa's cinema.

'If you see how dem boys does be rushing to mash up de place. An is for dem, you know. Is dem same niggars does be running to see any stupidness.'

As the second film began, a red cigarette butt went flying forward through the black from the back of Pit.

'What de fuck!'

A fight broke out. Shapes in the centre of Pit suddenly started flying around like on screen. They lunged together, knocking down benches. Lights came on and the film stopped. People jumped in, pulling the black kung-fu fighters apart as Ansa came running in, bravely waving his long arms about.

136

A huge woman grabbed Ansa's waist. 'All right, all right, all right. Dey done.'

She propelled him back outside. The crowd filed back in, lights went out and the movie continued.

After that, apart from a few farts causing ripples in Pit, the rest of the movie slowly got hazy as we started falling asleep on each other's laps and shoulders. Blurry-eyed down the steps, and a cool breezy sleepwalk home.

Mrs DeAbro watched Mikey passing in his uniform. She didn't say a word. None of her boys not joining nuthing.

'An' you believe some people sen'ing dey girl-chi'ren to join too? Some nice-nice girls, getting rough-up like boys, Mums.'

Mikey had joined the People's Militia. Got a brown uniform with a broad black canvas belt and black Army boots and was training to use a gun. Neighbour Mildred so proud of him, behaved as if he had gone off to fight a war, become a hero. But the base was right near town. And after he finished training there, he'd be back home, only reporting for practice sessions. I don't know what they was practising for. He and a couple other fellars had joined. Some of the big men was already in the Army or police force. Some teenagers from Tamarind Grove Secondary School joined the National Service and got bright green hats and uniforms and dark green boots. Boys and girls the same. From the time they put on that outfit after school and came down the road to train in the Primary School yard, they started behaving like different people. Like they didn't know us any more. Like they didn't have to listen to their parents. Like they didn't live in them houses in them side streets any more. Now they training to use a gun. First they had to march and we watched through the chainlink wire while they drilled for hours in the dust.

People start turning on each other more. The fellars who didn't join them PNC forces started listening to more Bob Marley. Some turned Rasta but then was war with they mothers. And all them uniforms didn't seem to bring no good, everybody in them was Burnham's men – they could go around terrorizing they own neighbour with guns.

'Why we can't go and play outside after eating?'

'Look out there. You see any small children running around? You see any girls walking? Youall just stay inside.'

'I still don't see why we can't just go outside for a little while now.'

'Look!' Sammy pointed. 'Dere's some scooter boys.'

They skewed past in a flash, four of them, hopping and crouching, left foot kicking on the asphalt.

'Please, please!'

'All right! All right! One hour.'

Me and Sammy shot over to DeAbro's, new rollerskates thumping on our backs.

'Judy! Rachel! We got one hour.'

Mrs DeAbro appeared with them. 'Youall parents let you out?'

'Yeah, yeah, hurry!'

We knew Mrs DeAbro trusted Mums's and Dads's

judgement on these things. Unlike them, though, she'd sit on that verandah and would be watching every time we passed her section of road. She'd be sitting in the dark, grumbling and worrying till Judy and Rachel came back home.

We sat down on the log across the road from some fellars liming, and laced up our prized rollerskates – the only ones in the village. Skew . . . skew . . . skew . . . the scooter boys flew past us on their iron wheels. Looked easy but only them boys could ride like that. Just two pieces of wood held in an L by a wire pin, running on ball-bearing cases from old cars. We watched them scooting past at breakneck speed – shoulders hunched, shirts flying, one foot pounding the road. They'd crouch with both feet on and make it hop – the whole scooter whirring. Or cruise with one foot lolling to the side, grind to a stop and spin round the back wheel in the gravelly edge of the road. The tumbles and bruises them boys could take if a stone chocked the front wheel. And get up and go again. They always tried to make us fall, skewing in close to our heels before swerving to the side. When we first got the skates we was wobbling about on them with the scooter boys round us jeering and begging for a go. But we practised under the house till we could stop and turn around, even do a little spin.

We tottered on to the road and set off. My legs felt like matchsticks with huge weights on the ends. Looked ridiculous, but was rollerskates and we had them first. The sound of hard plastic on the gritty asphalt cleared the cool night air for us to come sailing through. Up and down the road. Past the fellars watching. Past Mrs DeAbro craning. Up to Miss Isaac's house and turn. Passing back again. Breeze on your face, clothes fluttering behind, swinging slowly from foot to heavy foot – tall sailing mantises. We cruised up to the empty butcher stall and turned. About the third time we reached the stall, we realized something was going on by Mainroad. But Mainroad was out'a bounds for us at night. We sailed back down past the fellars. They had stiffened now, everybody standing. They weren't watching us. Turn by Miss Isaac's, come back down.

Clinton came hurrying in from Mainroad. Hustling along the edge of the road with his shades on, he swerved past the fellars.

'Clinty, wha happening?' one a'them shout out.

'Un hunh,' he grunted.

'Wha happening out by Mainroad?'

But he had already disappeared up the dark street. We skated up to the stall and turned around slowly, craning and cocking ears to catch what was going on. Back down. We stopped in front of DeAbro's shop. Suddenly, the road lit up and headlights roared towards us.

'Run!'

We stumbled off the road to the grass, clunking towards our gate.

'Is now we dead!'

The fellars scattered. The jeep slammed to a stop and the back doors burst open, tumbling out bout five policemen with guns and batons. Mrs DeAbro screamed. The fellars was fast. They melted out of sight before we could scramble through our gate and grab on to the van parked under the house. The policemen sniffed around where the fellars had been, like dogs that had lost the manicou. Then piled back into the jeep. In the front, young Constable Adams was sandwiched between the driver and another policeman. As the jeep lurched forward then jerked into reverse, he kept his head straight, not looking for anybody. Dark-road secrets starting to come out now.

'Oh me Lawd! What dem fellars do?' Mrs DeAbro was tirading to Mums next morning. 'Since de Pastor wife get rape and murder – you see what t'ings reach to, Rose? You 'ave to stay in you house. You can't even go outside. Wait till I see dat Adams! People ain do nuthing, an' police just locking dem up! Is money dey want! Tomorrow is court day. Dat's what Mrs Sampson say – she son get ketch by Mainroad last night. An' if you don' pay dem, you have to go to court. Get charge fuh *idling*! You ever see anyt'ing so? Oh Jesus Christ 'ave mercy! An' you know what, Mums? Dey will shoot somebody. Before long . . . dey will shoot somebody boy-child.'

'You know dat Miss Isaac's grandchi'ren going New York?'

'Who? Floydy and Toady?'

'Un hunh. Dat same liver-lip Floydy. And Toady.'

'Toady really eat cow poop for money?'

'Of course, plenty time. Bernard tell me so. Uncle Bonnie sendin fuh dem. Rememba he?'

'Yeah. He wid he flop-hat. He was de one dat started calling my father "Dads" an Mum "Mums" – tryin' to talk English like we.'

Judy smiled, remembering Uncle Bonnie. We walked along the warm seawall slowly against the breeze.

'Imagine he, working in New York! He couldn't even work de rotovator, the t'ing pull him all over de garden, mash-up all Dads's corn.'

Sammy and Rachel climbed up and over the seawall, down to the sea side. Tide was in. Brown water licking gently at the concrete slope. They nosed around, then scrambled back up to sit with us on top the wall.

'Yuh t'ink Miss Isaac would go?' Rachel asked.

'Go an leave she house an cows an everyt'ing?'

'I don know. How she go look after dem?'

None of us said anything.

'Felix said he goin' send for me,' Rachel announced.

Judy looked at her in disgust. 'Dat's why you was always stick-up next to him.'

'You would go an leave us?' Sammy asked.

'Well all your sisters gone an leave youall,' said Rachel.

'Dey *came* from Away, stupidy,' Judy answered. 'Anyway Felix ain sendin fuh you. He have three chi'ren up dere now.'

We were silent for a while. Sammy turned, lay down on her stomach and dangled an arm down the seawall alongside our legs.

'When we start Secondary School, we'll still lime together, right?' I said to Rachel.

'Un hunh.'

'We have plenty more years together, right?' Sammy put in.

'You soundin like a old lady already,' Judy growled.

'Rememba what you was talkin bout? We could get jobs in town and live in an apartment, like real town-girls.'

'Yeah, den we could do all dem wild-up t'ings.'

'An' have boyfriend an' t'ing!'

'Wha kind'a boyfriend you want?' Sammy asked Rachel.

'Oooh . . . a nice one. He mus have blond curly hair and blue eyes . . . an' red lips.'

'Aye! What you think you is! A white girl?'

'Is a movie star yuh lookin for? Go cinema, you'll find plenty! Look on all dem posters an' t'ing.'

'Wha kind you want, Sammy?'

'One like Raphael but younger. He like me, yuh know.'

Raphael was the handsome rich town-boy who turned vegetarian and started growing dreadlocks. He was a friend of the family, came and stayed with us sometimes to get away from town. When he came he had everybody in the village looking at him with a funny light shining in they eyes. Thoughts about 'nasty Rastas' disappeared. Even Mrs DeAbro liked him. He towered over everybody with his gold-skinned self, smooth forehead and perfect teeth. And a body and profile like out of one of them art books with white statues in them.

'He!'

'Umm,' Sammy said dreamily.

I knew then that Sammy's she-self had more power than I could ever get near. It was something I shouldn't try to copy or compete with. She couldn't help it. The minute Raphael was around, or Shaka the green-eye Rasta, she'd be sitting on they knees, climbing on they backs, up underneath they armpit, blinking her she-self eyes at them. Raphael only smiled vaguely at me – sneaking past with my book and feeling ashamed then of having no shirt and my father's old pants on. Was only once I talked with him – when I went for a walk by myself and found him on the bridge across Forty Canal.

I told him bout what I was reading – how people can communicate with each other without talking. But also if you listen, you can hear the whole Universe talking. Told him how I tried it and it worked. I was on my way to the seawall to sit and hear the clouds talking. He could hear them too if he tried. The best part is when the whole sky, the blue part and the sun, join in. And sunset time, when it starts getting all mixed up, changing voices and colours, when Breeze sings softly. On a good evening, the Egrets flying home and the Courida trees join in. Was close to the bombing-up exploding feeling. But I didn't know how to explain that to him.

Told him how in the night, from the upstairs window, the silver tops of the coconut trees talk to me. They swish and sway and whisper with scratchy voices. Their sharp edges glittering on big-moon night. A trance, the book called it. Trance-indental Meditation. It said you could just raise up off the ground, out of yourself, and take off, gone. I told him how I sit on big-moon nights, in that kind of trance thing, eyes wide open, and dream of flying over the sea of silver coconut trees. Swooping and playing with the bouncy clouds, looking down on the white streets and zinc sheet roofs of the sleeping village. Listening, from up there, to the little night-time sounds – a dog's bark, the frogs' chorus. Feeling the moonlight on my skin, rippling like water. Rolling around in it. All of that I told him. Never talked so much to anyone bout all that. Talked till the light was almost gone from the sky.

While I was talking, there on the springy-plank bridge over Forty Canal, he was looking far away. Listening and gazing. He turned to me when I finished.

'That's beautiful, Lula,' he said in a strange voice.

He looked at me, his eyes strange too, making me soft and jellyish.

'You're very . . . *mature* for your age.'

The jelly-soft feeling swelled up in me, warmed me right up to my ear-tips and stayed there while we walked back home together. We walked close-up, my arm brushing his thigh, down the just-dark street.

*

I turned to the girls on the seawall now. 'You all know what Raphael said to me?' I looked at Sammy. 'Said that I'm very *mature* for my age.'

'Wagh! An' you like dat?'

'How you mean? What?'

'You know what dat *mean*?' Judy half shouted. 'You *force-ripe*!'

'No!'

'Yes! Like dem town-girls. Dey *mature*. Force-ripe. Wagh!'

I didn't say nuthing. We just sat there on the wall some more, jiffling around. Judy didn't want to talk bout what kind of boyfriend she wanted. And because she was how she was, we couldn't press her. She just longed-out her Qwukwani mouth and said she 'ain looking fuh no man'.

'But you like André,' Sammy caught her.

Judy's head spun round. 'Wha de hell you talkin bout?'

'I see you already!' Sammy said, sneaky-like.

'Where? Where you can see me? Doing what?'

'I see you talkin to him by de shop de other night.'

'So what? I can't talk to people?' Judy steupsed and turned her long mouth back to the sea.

Rachel looked at her sister closely.

'Wha you watchin' me so for?'

André was a short dark boy from Scheme. He could be a man but he looked like he was born to stay young, quiet, so it was hard to tell his age. He didn't show off his man-self round the place. And he was always well dressed with them baggy pleated pants and proper shoes. His short-short hair was always shining, set in tight waves, and he had a thick gold chain, a wristband and matching ring. Talked in a soft smooth voice. I could see why Judy liked him. He had the smooth-face, gentle-eyed, sexy soul singer type of man-self.

147

His hands were clean, his nails pink and filed. He could be as neat and delicate as he wanted and nobody would doubt his man-self, because of the sex-look in his eyes.

Mrs DeAbro had watched him from her verandah when he came into Tamarind Grove.

'Whey he come from? He from Scheme? You can't trust nobody from Scheme. You see how he moving easy-easy so? Easy snake does bite hot.'

He'd stand by the shop and talk with Bernard.

'Whey he get dat gold chain from? How he always dress up so, hunh? Is drugs he dealing in. Have to be.'

Judy was standing next to her.

'He family have a big house, Mammy.'

'Oh ho? Big house nuh! I don't trust he. He too nicey-nicey all de time.'

Rachel was still inspecting Judy. Working it out. You could see her holding on to this news bout André. Storing it up to tell Emelda when she wanted.

TEN

The power of the PNC was everywhere and Burnham's face was everywhere. He smiled from lampposts and walls, from banners across roads, from over people's heads in every office and school. Always the same picture, cropped around the double chin so the beaming flesh was like a rubber stamp. Stamped into every Comrade's brain. PNC paunches, jowls and fat arms were stamps of his approval too. Every occasion had to start with the national anthem. Got so bad that even in the dark of the cinema no one dared to stay seated while it blared out. You felt that someone was watching and waiting to report you. Make you join the People's Militia or National Service or do 'voluntary' self-help labour in the hot sun.

I went past Burnham's country residence twice every day in the TATA school bus. The big shuttered front, the tall Royal Palms and well-kept hedge, made you look for something out of place. The sight of the Residence swept over you together with the first rush of sea breeze and rice fields after leaving Tamarind Grove. Opposite the house on the other side of the road, the helicopter pad made a solid black square in the moving green patchwork. Sometimes, the helicopter bringing Burnham from town made us bend and crane in the bus like the rippling rice blades. But no matter how hard I looked, I never saw anything unusual or sinister. Couldn't get a glimpse of the front garden pond with the Caiman Alligators in it. Even when Mrs Burnham's arm was broken (by Him), I didn't see any change in the pattern of half-open Demerara windows or in the positions of the guards.

When I entered Secondary School at thirteen, it was the first time in my life I wore a uniform. All the years being taught at home, it was the thing I had envied most. Even though Mums said that children who had to wear them hated their uniform, and maybe I'd hate it too if I had to wear it every single day, I thought it was a damn good thing. I going to be just like every other child in the school. We, the uniformed ones, would be invincible, a clan, a force to be reckoned with. I going to belong and it don't matter if I Indian, black or Dougla, if I fat or fine, that uniform would make me one of them. I could do anything and somebody wearing the same uniform would back me up. The school's world of breezy corridors, fancy labs and cool classrooms would be my territory. Me and a thousand others like me.

I agreed with my mother that the thin brown cotton fabric would be cooler than the synthetic gabardine that the girls used to make their dresses and skirts. And that it probably was the right shade of brown – they wore all shades of brown. But that first morning, standing in line with the whole school, my dress was red. On top of being more red than brown, it was baggy and shaky, changing shape with the breeze, instead of being stiff and smooth like everybody else's. Felt as red, hot and skinny as I looked but Mums had already made three dresses, all exactly the same. After a term had passed, when everyone was forgiving me for the shade of my brown dress, I moved up to form four where all the girls wore skirts and white shirts, not dresses. But my dresses were still new and I had to wear them for at least another term. And answer to new names – Fling-up an Clap, Spokes, Cripsy Biscuit.

In our schoolworld Mr Brown the headmaster was Forbes Burnham. Had the same smirk too. To prepare for the glorious future of self-sufficiency, Mahaica Secondary and plenty other schools over-equipped with Chinese aid were built to promote agriculture and vocational skills. But just like in the nationworld, agriculture became a punishment. The school garden never produced. Battalions of students in white socks, white shirts, well armed with spades, cutlasses and forks, turned dry soil eternally in the day's hottest sun. Trying not to sweat too much, we plucked uselessly at the nutgrass while the young teacher directed from the shade. We had everything – the land, water, equipment, seeds – but no expertise or desire. Like in the nation, productivity was zero. It was one of our small triumphs. Even the teacher didn't want to produce. None of us would benefit even if we did. And it made no difference, as long as you went through the motions. We wasn't any different to the government workers – like Guyana Electricity Corporation men. They stood there, six of them looking up the pole, all dressed up, one up the pole, three in the back of the truck listening to a radio, the driver sleeping – all getting paid a full day's wage. The only thing that 'produced' in our school was the chickens, you couldn't stop them anyway.

As the PNC man, Headmaster Burnham took it as his personal duty to embarrass non-PNC teachers, mostly Indian ones, in front of us. There was a skinny, mousy maths teacher who he'd terrorize so much she shook when he was near her. He'd get as close as he could, look at her arse and raise his eyebrows at us and then exclaim how he'd have to 'squeeze' to get out of there. Some of the men teachers stuttered and sweated when he was in the classroom.

He made you aware of his power all the time. He smiled at me, sly, knowing I came from a non-PNC home – maybe even WPA. I looked right back at him like my body didn't exist, refused to show any signs of being scared or intimidated by his lecherous looks. He'd stand in one of the long corridors that ran the length of the school, just watching, making sure everything was going smoothly. And he'd watch you walk towards him, aware that the breeze was pressing the dress material against your body and that your thighs kept marching out against it, pointing to where your crotch is. Had to hold your books in front of your hips. Or if you had shaking bubbies, hold the books up against them to go past him. And then you'd feel the back of your knees burning where the dress ended. I'd seen him holding big girls' hands in his gold-ringed ones while telling them off softly or congratulating them, they hanging their heads and twisting their feet. I wasn't going to give him that chance. The fact is he most probably never wanted to get me into his office, meagre skin-and-bones that I was. The girls with tight shirts and big busts and women with round behinds was what got his most drooling looks. When my mother came to school a couple of times to see him, he would watch her walk out to the car park, making sure I saw him watching her arse.

154

'**O**h Lord, Mums! Rose! Is why dey taking you to de station? Rose!' Mrs DeAbro hold on to her head and start bawling.

People coming at a run. The police waiting for my mother to get into the jeep.

'Adams! How you could do dis!' Emelda grip on to Constable Adams's forearm and start shaking him.

'Is OK, Emelda. Is all right. I have to go to the station cause dey found some foreign money in de house.' Mums's face was calm but the flesh under her chin trembled.

Emelda still gripping Adams's arm. 'But Dads just come from Away, Friday night. You didn't tell dem, Mums?'

'Yes. Yes Emelda. He forgot to take it to the bank this morning. Don't worry, is OK. Loose him, Emelda. Just watch the children for me till Dads reach back.'

'Yan, you go wid you mother.' Emelda pushed Yan into the back of the jeep.

Adams climbed in next to Mums, shut the door and the jeep roared off. Mrs DeAbro clamped on to her head again, bawling louder.

'Oh Lawd, Mammie, ssh.' Rachel hushed her and we steered her inside.

Miss Isaac and Mrs Sampson came puffing down the road from opposite directions. 'Wha happen? Wha happen to Mums?'

'Police came to our house, to search for "Arms and Ammunition" and "Political Propaganda" . . .'

'Wha's dat?' Emelda screeched.

'Opposition pamphlets and stuff. And drugs dey was looking for.'

'Drugs! Oh Lord God!' Emelda bawling fresh.

When the jeep stopped that morning in front our gate, we were upstairs clearing away breakfast. A big-mouth Corporal told Mums that they had a warrant to search the house.

'Search? What you mean search?'

'Yes ma'am. We have a warrant here to search de premises.'

Mums looked past him to the sheepish Adams still sitting in the jeep.

'Come in. You'll have to take off your shoes here though. We don't allow shoes in the house.'

The Corporal looked at her as if she was joking. She was figuring how to handle this best. It was Dads that usually insisted on that rule.

'No. Sorry we don't. It's OK, the dogs won't eat them.'

The Corporal and the other officers struggled to get their big black boots off.

Mums took the lead. 'One of youall start downstairs. The rest come with me.'

Yan was standing in the empty bottom-house. Dads had taken the van into town first thing that morning.

'Yan, you go with that officer.'

The Corporal and the others finally got their boots off and, as they trailed up the stairs, some big white footprints were left behind from the Corporal's big powdered socks. He stamped at the top of the steps, sending up a small cloud. Sammy, Saskia and me were still glued on to the windowsills.

'OK, girls. I want each of you to stay near one of these gentlemen. Show them where things are and just keep an eye on them.'

We didn't know why, but we started keeping an eye on them. Saskia gave them her most bull-cow look.

Mums turned to the policemen. 'Gentlemen. Two of you can start upstairs, bedrooms up there, and two of you on this floor – more bedrooms, kitchen and living room here.'

Miss Mary came running out of the kitchen. 'Mums!'

'It's OK, Mary, these gentlemen are just having a look around.'

Miss Mary checked Mums's face and hurried over to her room.

Mums followed the Corporal around and I followed a stupidy-looking red one. He stood up under the twirling mobile with his lip hanging down, eyes going round and round.

'Wha's dat?' he asked me.

'A hanging star,' I said. 'It's a star, you see the shape?'

'Yeah, yeah,' he spluttered, and stumbled across the room to the corner with the magazines.

He looked into the aquarium. Watched the fish swimming about for a bit then picked up a paperback book and flicked the pages. I watched him closely. I glanced at the piles of *Gramma* newspapers from Cuba with their big red headlines. Mixed in between them was WPA bulletins and the *Catholic Standard*. They wasn't opposition papers? Propaganda? I had heard Dads saying something bout these Communist papers. Redman was digging through the pile now. Looking between the papers like he was looking for squashed geckos or dead cockroaches. Meanwhile, Corporal's trail of foot powder went all round the kitchen. Upstairs, Saskia flew into her room ahead of the officer and pulled out all her panties from her drawer. Spread them round the room. 'He eye open big!' she boasted after.

Downstairs, Yan was leading the tour of the three rooms. In the middle room was Dads's collection of seeds, cuttings and herbs.

'That's a herb,' said Yan.

'Herb?' The officer sprang into life. 'Wha kind'a herb?'

'I don't know the name of it, is to make tea.'

He sniffed at the dried bush and, disappointed, put it down. Opened the small fridge. It was full of beancurd, small plastic bags with all kinds of seeds and some film. His eyes open wider.

'Wha's dis?'

'What?'

'Dese packets.' He pointed to the beancurd.

'It's called tofu. Is made from soya beans. You eat it.'

'You eat dat!' He picked up a packet of the white meat and slapped it over in his palm. 'Whey you get it from? Eh?'

'We make it.'

'Oh ho.' As if that explained why it was so strange-looking. He fumbled around and felt all the little bags of seeds.

'Why youall keep dat dere for?' He pointed to the rolls of film while closing the fridge door.

'Dey does spoil if you keep dem outside.'

'Humf. Wha's dis? Eh heh!' He grabbed a small bag of starch that was sitting on top the fridge. Squeezing it, rolling it with his thumb.

'That's cassava starch,' Yan answered quickly.

'Youall have cocaine?'

'Cocaine? No sir.'

'Marijuana?' The officer span around at Yan.

'No sir.'

'Oh ho!' He strolled through to the next room.

Back in the living room, the Corporal was inspecting the big bookshelf. He fished out some spectacles and twisted his head sideways to see the titles.

'Ah hah!'

Mums's eyes landed on it before his did – the bills of English money weighted down with coins.

'What's dis?' He picked them up, chucking the coins in his left hand.

'You can see what it is,' Mums replied.

'Don't you know is illegal to have foreign currency in your house like dis? What you doing with dis?'

Mums explained that Dads had come back in on Friday night and meant to take it to the bank first thing this morning.

'But he hasn't.'

'He forgot it and he reach in town already now.'

'All foreign currency must be changed within forty-eight hours.'

'I know that. Look, you can see his passport, he only came in on Friday night.'

'This is the t'ing. Sorry ma'am. You'll have to come down to the station to sort this out.'

Constable Adams came slinking down from upstairs, with his head down.

'Nuttin down here . . .' the one from downstairs reported, 'only a lot of funny-looking stuff.'

My Redman was hypnotized by the mobile again. Mouth open, eyes rolling.

Mums's face getting into that jeep was what made Emelda start screeching. Made my insides screech too. Sammy holding on squeezing the top of my arm. Saskia, so bold-face inside the house, took one look at Emelda and the people running down the road and started screaming 'Mammie! Mammie!' Mums's movements were jerky as she held on to the dashboard and pulled herself up into the jeep. As she looked at my eyes, then Sammy's, then at Saskia jumping around screaming on our bridge, her round face was trying to reassure us, make it all right. But her eyes wasn't all right, something in them had snapped, glassy now, storming up inside. Now she was going to the same dark dingy station in Cove & John where beat-up t'iefs and jeeploads of arrested fellars were taken.

'What de hell wrang wid dis place?' Mrs Sampson plunked herself down on the steps next to Emelda. She sat there, her huge arms trembling, shaking her head slowly. Miss Isaac was wringing her bottom lip and twitching about in front of us. And Emelda still groaning like she having another Breakdown.

ELEVEN

Two shots rang out. Then a burst of bullets. Half-past
nine in the night. We jump out'a bed. Fellars came
running in from Mainroad and others running out to
see. Feet pounding on the road.

'Police!' someone shouted.

They drive off already.

'Somebody geh shoot?'

'Nah. Dey ain ketch he, he run.'

Me and Sammy pelt out'a the house after Yan. Rachel and
Anne-Marie running out of their yard. Judy must be up
ahead already – she could run fast. Bernard came out of the
shop with Ricardo behind him doing up his pants. Pickey
Hair Ras and his friends milling around in the crowd of
people gathering at the top of the road. Mothers looking for
their sons. Bottom House Crappo scrambling her tray,
pushing her way through.

Other people came running towards us down from the
bridge by Scheme, from where the shots had blasted.

163

'Who geh shoot? Who geh shoot?'

'Dey ain ketch nobody.'

A car started blowing its horn to come through the crowd. I spotted Judy as the car lights broke a way through. It was her! It was her, running *back* from the bridge. She ran half-crouched under the big saman tree and along the school fence towards us then cut across the back of the gas station.

'Dat's not Judy?' Rachel gripped my arm.

I nodded. You couldn't mistake her, the only white skin in the crowd, caught in the car lights. Coming from the bridge! Anne-Marie caught her by the back of the gas station. Judy screamed. Ricardo cut it short with a hand clamped over her mouth, pulling her away from Anne-Marie. Everyone was looking at Judy now as Ricardo pushed her down the street, one hand squeezing the back of her neck. Mrs DeAbro was now rushing out clutching her flying nightie. When she spotted Judy and Ricardo, she turned and ran wailing into their yard. Ricardo dragged Judy up the stairs and pitched her on to the verandah floor.

'Emelda, you deal wid dat,' he growled and pushed past us, back out the gate to where the small crowd waited. 'Wha youall lookin' at?'

Some of the crowd hustled after Ricardo, back up the road. I saw Mikey there, turning to head home.

'Get up!' Shouted Anne-Marie.

Judy cringed tighter into a ball, growling and sobbing on the verandah floor. Anne-Marie grabbed her foot and started pulling her inside the house. We grabbed on to Anne-Marie's clothes to stop her, Judy kicking with her other foot, holding on to her head still. We could hear Emelda thrashing about inside, looking for the wild cane.

'What . . . you . . . was . . . doing . . . out . . . *dere*!' Wild cane came lashing out.

The blows fell on Judy everywhere as the front door slammed shut behind us.

'Mammie!'

'No, Mrs DeAbro! No!' We grabbed on to Emelda's feet.

'Get off! Loose me!' She drop a lash on us. 'Out! Youall go home! Home!'

'Mrs DeAbro. . .'

'OUT!' She lashed the door next to my face and rammed it shut.

'What . . . you . . . was . . . doing . . . out . . . *dere*?' The cane ripped down on Judy curled on the floor, kicking and blocking her face.

'Aye! Aye Mammie aye!'

Rachel screaming 'Mammie! Mammie!'

Me and Sammy paste-up together outside on the verandah. Mikey hadn't gone home. He stood silhouetted by the electricity pole just outside the fence.

'Mammie! Mammie! Aye, aye aagh . . .' Judy started screaming like a pig.

'What de fuck you was doing, eh?' Wild cane struck.

'You supposed to be inside, eh.' Two strokes.

'Everybody inside. An' where you? By Scheme. By SCHEME!'

The lashes, screams and thumps on the floor got faster.

'*Scheme!* Dey should'a shoot *you*!' She kicked Judy's legs.

'What de hell you was doing? Eh? Eh?' She dropped down on her knees and shook Judy.

A new voice came out Emelda's throat. A deep growl we'd never heard before. 'You better tell me Judy. Or believe me, I go break every bone till you talk.'

165

Judy silent.

Emelda jumped up again. 'You went to meet *him*, eh? *He*! Dat black good-fuh-nuthin! What . . . you . . . want . . . wid . . . *he*? Eh?'

'Aye, Mammie, aye! We was just talkin, Mammie.'

'Talking! Talking! You creeping out'a de house to go an' *talk*! Is Man you want, eh Judy. Is *Man* you want? De *police* should'a hold you, den you would'a see. Where you was lie-down taking he, eh? Eh?'

'We was in de bus shed . . .'

'*Eh!*'

' . . . talkin! Mammie . . . talkin.' Judy sounded weak.

Emelda rushing round the room now, lashing the furniture with the wild cane.

'Oh *God*! *My* daughter dere taking black man in de bus shed! Oh Lord! God, you have no mercy on me! *Taking man!* When people frighten to go outside, you dere *taking man by de roadside*!'

'We was talk . . .' A lash came down on her head and arms.

Emelda lashed it out of Judy. It seemed like for ever. People on the road started moving away. But Mikey stayed and me and Sammy stuck on the verandah. We could hear Mums calling us from our kitchen window.

I could imagine Judy and André flying out of the bus shed when the police raid broke out. The fellars liming on the bridge streaking along the bank towards Backdam before the police opened fire. Judy and André scrambling down into the bushes at the other end of the bank. Slipping into the mud clutching on to each other. But even then, the fear of being caught ringing louder in Judy's ears than the bullets.

*

'You taking man, eh! You is a big woman to take man, eh. Eh!'

'No Mammie! Mammie!'

'In de bus shed like a whoa! *Black Man!*'

'No Mammie!'

'No? No?' She grabbed Judy by the hair, dragging her across the room. 'No? How long now you openin yuh legs fuh he?'

'No Mammie . . . aagh . . .'

Emelda slapped her loud. 'You still sayin no! Judy. . .watch me! You telling me you wasn't dere spreading yuh legs in de bus shed? Is how he had you? Brace-up, stand-up? Lord, God, Father! You can't lie to *me* you know!' Her voice cracked.

Judy was hunched against the wall shaking her head, dribbling and gagging on her in-breath. 'Nooo. . .'

'Judy. . .watch me. He beat you to make you not talk?' Judy jerking still.

'Is rape, you know. Black man does rape . . . *but he can't rape you if you get away to go an' take it!!*' She dropped the wild cane and jumped down on her, Judy fighting back.

'You raisin yuh hand at *me*? Anne-Marie, come!'

Anne-Marie dropped Rachel and grabbed Judy's hands. Mrs DeAbro sat on Judy and slapped her face. Over and over and over.

'Agnes! Come here! Hold one foot.'

Agnes came and gripped one ankle, tears running down her round face. Judy stopped twisting and lay groaning.

'Mammie, no! What you doing? Mammie!' Rachel sobbed softly, not moving from where she was.

'I goin see what you was doing!' She started pulling up Judy's skirt, tugging at her panty.

'Yuh can't hide nuthing from me. *You.* Yuh lying little whoa. I always suspect you. *Blight!*' She got the panty off one foot, Judy not resisting. Pushed open her legs. 'Agnes, look!'

Agnes's head was down, shaking. Anne-Marie looking from on top. Emelda pushed her head closer, fixing her glasses. '*Red!* Why you crease red? *Red!*'

Rachel opened the door and crept out on to the verandah with us. Mikey was still standing there. As we looked at him, he slowly turned and moved silently into the dark end of the street. We sat down right there. Couldn't believe Mrs DeAbro would do that. Couldn't believe Judy would do that. She been doing it all the time with André. Didn't tell us nuthing. Now the whole village knew.

The Buxton Spice was watching. Not saying nothing, just breathing hard. Breathing hard and watching every move. I watched it back. It scrubbed its knuckles on the galvanize roof, trying to say something. I sat on top the big bookshelf passing down books for packing. Mikey was helping us lift the boxes. I handed the 'Black Albino' painting to Mums.

'And the other one too, dear.'

I passed the oil painting down, the scary one that haunted me every time I came down the steps to the bathroom at night.

The Buxton Spice scratched and grumbled.

'What de hell you grumbling bout? We have British Passport, we don't have to stay! All dese years we here, you know bout t'ings and wouldn't tell me nuthing. You the one always spying. Well we goin now! You could stay and watch people suffer more. You could take over de whole house. Spread out yuh fat feet and break open de septic tank!'

It dangled a fat rosy mango.

'What you swinging dat at me for now? You never give me none before. You can drop yuh stinking mangoes all over now.'

I watched it hanging there though, just outside the window. A square of late afternoon light slanted in. The tree swayed, rumbled its deep laugh. I knew it was watching Mikey's bare back bent over a box of books. The two smooth long muscles on either side of his spine tightened as he straightened up. A soft shadow stroked along his back, dipping in to his narrow waist.

Mikey turned, caught my eye and winked. 'I could come wit' youall?'

I winked back. 'Come nuh!'

The Morris chairs gone, in the back of the truck, leaving square ghosts in their places. The patch of dull floor grinned at me, free now to feel the soles of feet on its skin – Tibisiri mat rolled-up and gone.